T0375648

Right as Church on Sunday Morning/ New Beginning

Susan Beard Istre

WESTBOW
P R E S S®
A DIVISION OF THOMAS NELSON
& ZONDERVAN

WestBow Press books may be ordered through booksellers or by contacting:

WestBow Press
A Division of Thomas Nelson & Zondervan
1663 Liberty Drive
Bloomington, IN 47403
www.westbowpress.com
844-714-3454

Scripture quotations are taken from the American Standard Version Bible (Public Domain).

ISBN: 979-8-3850-2392-9 (sc)
ISBN: 979-8-3850-2393-6 (hc)
ISBN: 979-8-3850-2391-2 (e)

Library of Congress Control Number: 2024908056

Print information available on the last page.

WestBow Press rev. date: 05/30/2024

Chapter 1

E mma Grace, along with her best friend Liz, rounded a corner and bumped into a tall, lanky, long-haired, skinny cowboy with a week's worth of facial stubble.

"Excuse me, ma'am," he said with a base-deep, raspy, and almost inaudible voice.

"Oh, excuse me. I'm sorry; not paying any attention," she quickly answered, somewhat embarrassed as she tried to stop the soft blush color she felt rising to her cheeks.

Alec Eli tipped his hat and walked on, but not before Emma Grace, for a brief second, felt his intense stare at her from his hypnotizing blue-gray eyes that made her catch her breath.

Before she could recover and make sense of what she had just felt, Will swaggered up alongside her friend, Liz, and Liz's husband Rick. Will shook Rick's hand, flashed his smile that could light up all of Texas, and so self-assuredly said, "Hey, buddy. How are ya? It's been a while." Will then turned his magnetic smile towards Emma Grace and said,"Hi. I'm Will, and you are?"

Emma Grace reached out to shake his hand but lost hers in his. With her heart in her throat, replied, "Emma Grace."

There was an instant electric charge that traveled through her body. His penetrating eyes had a sharp brilliant piercing and twinkle that captivated her.

Alec Eli Wagner tipped his hat and his usually hardened unsmiling face was for an instant brightened by an infrequent almost imperceptible soft smile he gave to the pretty young lady with the surprisingly brilliant green eyes that for an instant made him quickly catch his breath while hiding his self-inflicted anger. Any other time he would have stopped and flirted with this pretty lady he collided with regardless if he was involved with Scarlett or not. He was not a man who would pass up an opportunity to flirt with a pretty girl, and pretty girls came with the territory of being the American Bull Rider of the Year. But tonight was different; he had come away from this rodeo closer to the bottom than the top, and he didn't know what to do with that. He was riding through unfamiliar territory and emotions. In a rush to put this rodeo and tonight's ride behind him, he unsaddled Maggie, brushed her down, loaded her into the trailer with some hay, packed up his gear, kicked up a not so small dust storm of dirt and straw, cussed more than a few times, and at a reckless speed that mirrored his anger, bolted his truck and trailer out of the parking lot and headed towards the next rodeo and another ride. Tom and Matt were lucky to jump into the cab before Alec took off. Tonight he had drawn Mission Impossible, one of the hardest bulls to ride on the circuit, but he hadn't had a good ride all week. So tonight's fiasco wasn't entirely a surprise. In the truck, Alec went over every detail of his preparation and short ride over and over with Tom and Matt. No alarms or mistakes went off.

Eight hours later, with burning anger slowly rising to the surface, he, his brother Tom, and his friend Matt were in the next town ready for the next rodeo. It was best to get some breakfast and might as well have a beer, or two … or three with his eggs before getting some sleep and gearing up for the night's rodeo. Forget about Houston and start over here. It was still early in the season, plenty of time to still be in the running for the American Bull Rider of the Year again.

"Hey, you think that's smart to start drinking so early in the morning?" asked Tom.

Alec slowly drained the mug, met his brother's eyes and replied with just a touch of a dare. "Yeah." He pushed back his chair, turned his back on Tom and Matt, and with an overly confident air walked away.

Chapter 2

It was the Houston Livestock Show and Rodeo, and on this particular beautiful and chilly February night she and her best friend, Liz, and Liz's husband, Rick, and her new acquaintance, Will, walked through the stalls behind the rodeo arena.

As they walked, Emma Grace digested all the sounds and smells of the rodeo.

She loved the rodeo. She loved the animals and their untamed strength and wildness. She loved the beauty she saw in the unbroken horses. She loved the sounds of the crowds, the neighing of horses, the snorts of bulls, and the yelling of the cowboys. She loved the smells of fresh hay and the other pungent smells of a used barn. She loved the struggle between man and animal played out in the arena. Every event, every ride was a fight for domination. This was God's universe playing out in front of her eyes.

As the four of them walked and talked, it seemed Will knew everyone and everyone knew Will. The cowboys stopped, shook his hand, and called him, "Sir." He answered them back with a handshake, a slap on the back, a broad smile, and a voice that thundered throughout the stalls. He met each cowgirl with a hug (a little longer than Emma Grace thought necessary) and a kiss on the cheek.

"How are you sweetheart? Where have you been? I've been looking all night for you," thundered and echoed throughout the stalls, and Emma Grace noted, "Player and playboy" in her mind.

Will was older than she and working on his way to become a Texas Ranger. He was big with broad shoulders, penetrating brown eyes, and thick dark brown hair cut short and hidden most of the time beneath his white Stetson. He had a swagger that was full of arrogant confidence, rightness, bigness, and meanness. "You guys want to get something to eat before calling it a night?" Will asked them. Before she could reply, Rick answered, "Yes" for all of them.

The next day at the hospital where Liz and Emma Grace both worked as nurses, Liz pulled Emma Grace aside, "A word of warning, Will is a player. Don't take him seriously; he will break your heart. I've seen him do it more than once."

"Yeah, I got that feeling watching him last night greet the cowgirls," Emma Grace replied.

"Well, to Rick and I, the only people at the table last night were the two of you.

I'm just telling you to be careful."

"Thanks, but I got his number."

Before Emma Grace made it home after her shift at the hospital, Will called her on her phone. She was so excited to hear from him, she never found out how he got her cell number.

Will took her to an exclusive and fancy cozy restaurant in downtown Houston for their first date. Because exclusive and rich was the way Emma Grace was brought up, exclusive and rich did not impress her. What did impress her were his manners … impeccable: opening the car door, removing his Stetson indoors, standing up when she excused herself from the table, and pulling her chair out for her when she returned. "Don't forget he's a player", she repeatedly told herself.

At the restaurant, Will put his hand on the small of her back and gently guided her to their table in a quiet corner of the restaurant. In the soft glow of dimmed lights and candlelight, Will was softer and quieter than she remembered him from the rodeo.

"Champagne?" he courteously asked.

"Yes, please. Sounds good."

He turned to the waiter and ordered a bottle of champagne while pointing it out on the cocktail/wine menu. He handed the menu back to the waiter, turned his twinkling eyes to Emma Grace and asked with a broad smile, "How was your day?"

No one had ever specifically asked her how her day had been. Yes, she knew she was loved and people cared for her, but she couldn't remember anyone ever specifically asking her after a long day at the hospital how her day had been.

"It was good."

"Well, what did you do?"

"Oh, you really don't want to hear all the routine and mundane things a nurse does all day."

"Yes, I do. I think what you do is very interesting. The things you see, the things you do, the stories you have to tell, the lives you save. A wonderful and exciting gift you have."

"Thank you, but I'm sure my job is boring compared to your job of busting down doors, high-speed car chases, chasing down criminals, and facing life and death situations."

"It's really not as glamorous as you make it out to be."

"Neither is mine."

"Well, it seems we are both in the life-saving business, and we both find it dull and unglamorous."

Is he being sincere or mocking? He is a player. You know that, she told herself. You've seen him in action. But, his seemingly sincere care for her and his interest in her job, along with his impeccable manners and dreamy eyes left Liz's warning floating away along with Emma Grace's caution.

Will walked her to the door and softly kissed her goodnight. She fought hard against the desire to ask him in, praying for the courage to let him go. God answered, but in that instant leaning against the inside of the closed front door as Will walked back to his truck, Emma Grace knew she had totally and completely fallen in love, and for half a second wondered if she should talk this over with God.

Chapter 3

This rodeo didn't prove to be any better. Again, Alec came in closer to the bottom than the top. Tom tried to reassure his brother this was just an off-stretch he was going through; every rider went through it. He would find his sweet spot again, and everything would be fine. Keep studying, riding, focusing, and things would turn around.

They didn't. Through that spring and early summer, the harder Alec rode and the more he focused on another American Bull Rider of the Year title, the shorter the rides, the lower the scores, and the more meanness came out of Alec. Before long, Alec was spending more time in bars and more time with Scarlett than he was spending around bulls and arenas … until they finally rolled into Cheyenne.

Cheyenne was familiar territory and familiar crowds. He was home in Cheyenne. He could not remember there ever being a Cheyenne rodeo in which he had not participated, from taking care of the saddle and bareback broncs his family ranch bred for the rodeo circuit to eventually, when he was old enough and good enough, riding bulls. He loved coming back to and visiting the places where he, Tom, and Matt had shared so many good times. Here, in Cheyenne, the rides were longer and better; the crowds were louder and friendlier, the memories good and satisfying,

Alec needed this rodeo more than anything. He needed good rides; he needed to get back on top. He swore off drinking for this rodeo, and after a loud and violent scene with Scarlett, sent her packing. He spent all of his time-off watching videos of different bulls but especially videos of Rambunctious, the newest and wildest bull on the circuit. This bull had a reputation; no one had ever lasted eight seconds on him, and Alec wanted to be prepared for this bull. He wanted to draw him; he needed to draw him, so he spent countless hours studying the bull's rides. Did he lift his back-end first or front-end first? How did he come out of the chute? Did he spin to the right or the left? How many spins before he changed directions? Did he come up off all fours? What was his pattern? Did he have a pattern?

"Yes," he shouted out loud and gave high fives to Tom and Matt when he drew Rambunctious on the last night of the rodeo. A good ride on the unrideable Rambunctious and a little bit of luck could put him back on top.

Alec stood on the top steel rail on the backside of chute number four and studied the bull. Rambunctious bucked a few times and, to the gasps of the crowd, tried to climb over the gate. Alec waited for the bull to settle. After adjusting his vest, securely fastening his helmet, and pulling his gloves on tightly, Alec silently slung his leg over the top rail into the chute and slowly straddled the bull before gently finding the spot on the bull's back. He grasped the rope with his gloved left hand and wrapped it till he felt sure, settled further down into his sweet comfortable spot on the bull's back, balanced himself, put his free hand on the top of the gate, and gave a nod. The gate sprung open, but in his hurry to get out of the gate and throw the weight off his back, Rambunctious stumbled and slammed his full weight into the side of the chute crushing Alec's right side. While Alec tried to free his left hand from the rope thinking he would get a re-ride, Rambunctious found his balance and sprang out of the gate, slinging the off-guarded Alec off his back and into the dirt. Alec quickly and desperately tried to stand up and run from the charging bull, but his crushed right leg landed him back in the hard dirt just in time for Rambunctious to charge at him again and fling him through the air like throw-away trash. Again, the bull charged at Alec, but this time Matt, in clown make-up and a brightly colored polka-dot shirt, ran screaming towards the bull with arms flailing daring the bull to chase him to the top rail of the gate. Matt reached the top rail just as Rambunctious' hot breath blew on his back and the pick-up men rode up alongside the bull with their ropes circling in the air searching for the bull's horns. Rambunctious, seeing the pick-up men, stopped, swished his tail, snorted, and sauntered through the gate and back behind the chutes. A motionless Alec laid in the dirt.

The next day the reality of the busted ride was slowly seeping through Alec's consciousness before he ever opened his eyes, but it was the commotion down the hall that sprung his dazed and confused eyes open, and he knew the toxicity that was coming even before she entered the room. Even though he was still in a medicated haze, he could hear the teeth-grinding commanding volume of her voice and feel the chilling larger-than-life presence several doors down the hall before the ample-breasted and full-figured Scarlett strutted into his hospital room. If he could run, he would. But he was trapped; trapped by the bed rail, the IV taped to the back of his hand, and the open-backed hospital gown.

He had met Scarlett in a bar in Billings after he had wrapped up that rodeo with a first place finish in bull riding. He was drunk and pleased with himself; she was sassy and flirty. The connection was like lightning striking an electric transformer: bright, electric, flaming, and deadly. He quickly grew tired of her, but she scratched an itch for him, and he used her as much as she used him. It didn't matter how many times he broke it off with her, or she broke it off with him; she always came back, and now here she was.

"Hey, baby. I heard what happened, so I came as fast as I could. I'm here to help you in whatever way I can," she ordered as she marched into his hospital room, dropped down the bed rail, and plopped down on the edge of the bed with such force that the IV drip jiggled and Alec silently winced at the jarring.

"We broke up, remember? I told you to leave, " was the barely grunted reply from Alec.

"That was just temporary. I know you really didn't mean it," and she leaned over and gave him a long drippy wet kiss. "Admit it, you've missed me."

"Not really."

But Scarlett didn't take the hint and Alec didn't have the strength to fight, but his mind did go back to the last time he saw her: He was drunk as usual and she was sassy as usual. He tried to remember what that particular fight was about but only the verbal and physical onslaughts came to mind as well as the hazy hotel room, the bitter drunken night accompanied by the left-over taste of hard whiskey, her overpowering sickening sweet perfume, and her cigarette breath that burned into all of his senses the morning after. With that he realized he was at the bottom of the barrel, so he threw her out, sobered up, and cleaned up his act before the final night when he drew Rambunctious to ride.

"I'm Alec's fiance," Scarlett so boastfully declared to the nurse.

"Ma'am, did you see the 'No Visitors' sign on the door?"

"Did you not hear me? I'm Alec's fiance," was the sharp and snappy reply.

"Ma'am, the doctor's orders are 'No Visitors'. I'm going to have to ask you to leave. Please leave before I call security."

"Alec, tell her who I am and that you want me to stay."

"Scarlett, please go. I'm really tired and don't feel up to dealing with you right now."

"Oh, you don't mean that," Scarlett replied and then turned to the nurse and demanded, "Call security, the doctor, anybody that can override you."

Somewhat flustered, the nurse picked up the phone and began to call security just as Matt walked in.

"Matt, please tell this person who I am and that I have a right to be here next to Alec."

Jokingly, because Matt loved giving the much hated Scarlett a hard time, said, "Who are you?"

"Come on, Matt. Alec and I are engaged, and his fiance should be here for him."

"Fiance, I don't know about and since when have you ever been there for Alec? Alec, do you want her here?"

"No," was the deep-throated whispered but firm reply from a closed-eyed Alec.

Nurse, go ahead and call security; this woman doesn't belong here."

Security showed up, and Scarlett swung her large handbag over her shoulder, shouted, "I'll be back," through her bright red over-puffed lips and stomped out of the room.

"That woman with her big hair, big boobs, big voice, and big purse is bad news for Alec. Do NOT ever let her anywhere near him. Understand?"

"Mr. Wagner, is that what you want?"

"Yes," was the whispered but gruff reply.

"Yes, sir. I'll make a note in very large letters on your chart."

Hours later Alec again opened his eyes and tried hard to remember. As his eyes took in the sights, and he felt the touches of the sterile hospital room, reality slowly revealed itself to Alec. He felt something squeeze his left arm so tightly he tried to rip it off, but he couldn't move his right arm. He had broken his right shoulder when Rambunctious stumbled while bolting out of the gate, and his body was slammed up against the side of the chute. Not only could he not move his right arm, he also could not move his right leg; it was in a cast.

"How ya feel?" asked Matt as he quietly walked out of the shadows of the hospital room and up to his bedside.

A deep and low "Mmmmmm," was all Alec could moan while he tried to keep his eyes open and focus on the cold and sterile room filled with rhythmic machines quietly and frequently announcing he was still alive.

"The doctor will be in in a minute. Is there anything I can get you?"

Alec opened his mouth, "Did I dream that Scarlett was here, or was she really here?"

"She was here."

"Keep her away. I don't want …" the door to the room opened and the doctor walked in.

"How's the patient?" matter-of-factly the doctor questioned.

"He's awake."

A silent pause before the doctor spoke as if he was weighing what needed to be said next.

"Mr. Wagner, do you feel like you are awake enough to hear me and understand what I'm going to tell you about your injuries?

Alec nodded.

"Do you remember what happened?"

Alec stared past the doctor into the blank wall while foggy memories of the bull stumbling and then taking off like a rifle shot leaving Alec in the dirt came somewhat into his mind's eye. There were mind flashes of the gasps of the crowd, cowboys standing over him, bright lights of the hospital, people whispering around him, the sound of Scarlett's voice … that was it until now, so he gave a half nod and a slight shrug of his shoulders.

"Okay. Try to focus and listen carefully as I explain your injuries and what we did to put your leg back together. You with me, Mr. Wagner?"

A more perceptible nod from Alec, and his drug-clouded eyes did their best to zero in on the doctor's face.

"I don't exactly know how it happened, but the entire right side of your body was crushed, especially your right leg. Because of the weight of the impact, the damage was significant and could only be repaired with multiple screws and bolts. We had to remove some of your right shin bone; it was too shattered to correct, so now your right leg is somewhat shorter than the left. There will be some limp, but I thought the limp was better than losing the leg altogether. You are going to have to spend quite a bit of time in physical therapy, and in time there might be some medical breakthroughs and additional surgeries that will be able to put your right leg back together as good as it was before, but for now, this is all I could do to save your leg. In addition, your right collarbone along with your right arm were broken. You also suffered a concussion; I would not recommend riding anymore. Another accident could paralyze you permanently; another blow to the head could kill you. If there is any good news, it's that you are alive. I'm going to keep you here for a while and start your physical therapy. I'm not going to sugar-coat anything; you have a long road ahead of you, but you're going to be fine. Any questions?

Alec mouthed, "No."

I'll be back tomorrow. A pause, and then, "You are one lucky cowboy."

Alec closed his eyes, and Matt went back to his chair.

The longer Alec laid in that hospital bed, the farther he felt his life of riding bulls pull away from his grip just the way a dream can slowly retreat from one's memory no matter how hard one tries to hold it. The realization that he could not ride anymore brought new questions he had to wrestle with. Where would he live? How would he make a living? What to do about Scarlett? And what never left his mind: What would happen if he did start riding again?

The only option that came back time and time again to him was to move back to the ranch and recover. That meant … his dad. He would rather be anywhere than at the ranch with his dad. No, not true. He would rather go back and face his dad than live with Scarlett.

So, back to the ranch a discouraged and broken Alec went, bracing himself as best as he could for "I told you you'd amount to nothing."

The one bright spot was Tom and his four kids, especially the oldest one Luke, an untamed and fearless twelve year old boy who worshiped his Uncle Alec, were now living at the ranch. They had been Tom's sole responsibility since his wife, Kathy, abandoned him and the children a year ago; for where? Nobody knew. Kathy, Tom's wife and mother of his four children, left the house one day to pick up another pain-killing prescription and never returned. Tom spent considerable time, money, and resources to find her, but failed. Even her parents who lived in Arizona claimed they had not seen or heard from her.

Chapter 4

As that spring and summer passed with intimate romantic dinners, shooting dates at the gun range, and small town rodeos and street dances, Emma Grace fell deeper in love with the impeccable manners, the dreamy brown eyes, and the attention.

"Hey, Emma Grace, want to go for a quick drink?" Liz asked one summer day after their shift was over at the hospital.

"Sounds good. Let's make it short, though. Will and I are meeting my parents tonight for dinner."

"Okay. We'll make it short."

Settled across from each other in a booth at Chuy's for happy hour and after two margaritas with salt and chips and a large bowl of queso, Liz questioned, "How's Will?"

"Good. Great."

"How are things between the two of you?" asked Liz.

"Great. Couldn't be better. Why?" asked Emma Grace.

With hesitation in her voice, Liz began, " Emma, I'm going to be honest with you. You can either hate me or love me for this, but please keep in mind I love you like a sister, and I really only care about you; I want the best for you; I don't want you to get hurt."

"Okay. Shoot. What's up? Sounds serious."

"When Rick and I were in Austin last weekend, we saw Will at Pappadeaux's ... with another woman."

"Yeah, he was in Austin running another prisoner exchange. He has to do that quite often. Her name is Lisa; she's just a fellow agent."

"They seemed pretty friendly. Lots of laughing and familiarity with each other. I thought it would have been an embarrassing conversation, so we didn't go up and speak to him. I'm pretty sure he didn't see us."

"Well, you should have. They are just good friends. In fact, they talk to each other on the phone,"

"That doesn't concern you?"

"No. Why should it? If he were hiding something from me, he sure wouldn't tell me about her or talk to her on the phone in front of me. Listen, Liz, thank you for being so concerned. I appreciate it, and I know how you feel about Will. But, you're not there in our intimate pillow talks. You don't see the look in his eyes; you don't feel his tender touch; you don't hear the genuineness in his voice; you don't taste his tears when he breaks down and bears his soul to me. I do and because of that, I love and trust him."

"I don't trust him. I don't believe him."

"Why? Am I not good enough for him? Is it so hard to believe that someone like him could love me?"

"Don't be silly, of course not. He's not good enough for you. You're so much better than him. He doesn't deserve you."

"Maybe you're just being a little over-protective."

"Maybe. I still don't trust him. He's got a reputation."

"People can change."

"Maybe. Have you prayed about this?"

"Of course, I have," was the flippant response from Emma Grace. Besides, why would God allow this if it wasn't meant to be?"

"You know the answer to that. It's just that I think you've allowed your relationship with Will to take precedence over everything. You don't come to Bible Study anymore, and I rarely see you in church anymore. I'm worried."

There was an awkward pause with the waiter asking if there was anything else they needed.

"Just the check, please," was Emma Grace's response.

At last, "Okay. Just make sure God is in your relationship with

Will," was Liz's reply. "I care about you and don't want you to get hurt."

"I know, and I love you too."

Later on at dinner, Liz's words kept popping up in Emma Grace's head, "He's got a reputation"; "I don't trust him"; "They were laughing and very familiar with each other"; "Just make sure God is in your relationship with Will." This last statement bothered Emma Grace the most. God had always played an important part in her life. She was brought up going to church every Sunday, she prayed daily and had always put her faith and trust in Him, but since Will had entered her life, God had taken a back seat in the priorities of her life. She had replaced God with Will. But can't it be both, God and Will?

Just then, Will put his arm around her and drew her closer to him and placed a tender kiss on her forehead, the thoughts disappeared, and Will and dinner was as always. There was still the hand-holding and the squeeze of her hand every now and then to remind her that he was thinking about her. There were still the deep looks into her eyes, the smiles, and the "I love you's."

In the car on the way home from dinner, Emma Grace turned towards Will and asked, "How's Lisa?"

Will froze for a half blink of an eye, recovered more quickly than the freeze, shot a look at Emma Grace, and confidently replied, "I guess, fine. Why do you ask?"

"Oh, just wondering. You said you have another prisoner exchange run later this week, and I was just wondering how she was. She hasn't called in a while, and I thought you would probably see her again."

"I guess. She's usually the agent on the other end," was the casual reply.

Emma Grace turned back to the front and smiled. There. No red flags that she could see.

Many after- church family dinners with Will's family and Emma

Grace in attendance had become the norm, and on one of the last Sundays of the summer, Emma Grace's parents had been invited.

After the fried chicken and before the peach cobbler, Will unexpectedly took Emma Grace's left hand, knelt in front of her and asked, "Will you marry me?"

There were quite a few gasps that pulled the air out of the room for a brief second before Emma Grace broadly smiled and replied with an excited, "Yes."

There were shouts of congratulations, toasts, hugs, and kisses from both sides of the family. This was indeed a perfect match.

It wasn't long after the third finger on her left hand was newly dressed in a large beautiful diamond ring when Will charmingly and lovingly insisted she move in with him into his house in the country.

"It makes so much sense," he said. "Just think of the money we will be saving, supporting one household instead of two. Besides, we are going to be married. Let's go ahead and live together." He kissed her and smiled that smile that always made her melt.

She knew it wasn't right; it went against everything her faith had taught her, but Will had convincingly made it sound so simple and sensible that she gave in and moved in with him.

Of course there was now the job of telling her parents, and it played out just exactly as she knew it would. Her mother went into a lecture about how this was not what "our kind" of people did. We are not the kind of people that live "that" way. Now, he would never marry her. No one respectable (which meant "monied" and "churched" in her mother's eyes) would ever marry her now. Not only had she ruined herself, but she had also brought shame to her family. Her mother accepted Will just as long as he followed the old Southern and religious rules, but the minute the proper Southern protocols were broken and one of the deeply in-grained religious "can't do's" was broken, Will was no longer regarded as acceptable for Emma Grace. From then on her mother masked her disdain for Will behind proper Southern politeness, but she never let Emma Grace forget her true feelings. It made for uncomfortable family gatherings.

Daddy responded in his usual comforting way, "Don't worry about your mom. I've got your back."

Emma Grace could always count on her dad as an ally. In this instance, his "I've got your back" resulted in her Mom's proper Southern politeness. Family gatherings could have been a lot worse.

It wasn't her parent's reaction that bothered Emma Grace the most. It was her relationship with God. She knew what living with Will without a wedding ring meant. It meant she was going against her beliefs in God's teachings she had learned through all of the Sunday School lessons she had attended for almost all of her life. But surely God understood, she tried to convince herself. Things were different today. Just because they didn't have a marriage license didn't mean they weren't "married." They were married in mind, heart, and body, and she did have an engagement ring. God knew this and certainly He understood. After all, didn't God allow them to meet and fall in love? But still … She rolled over in bed that first night at Will's house, and the tears quietly ran down her cheeks and onto the unfamiliar smell of the pillowcase. She silently prayed and asked God for forgiveness. She knew God was telling her this was wrong; she felt the wrongness in her soul. This was not God's path for her, and she knew it, but what could she do now? She had made her decision. Will was worth it, and God would just have to keep forgiving her.

Living with Will was great. It was just like she always dreamed. They went their separate ways in the morning; she went to the hospital; he went to headquarters; and they both worked serving the community in their respective jobs. At some point during the day, Will called, and they made their plans for dinner. Sometimes they ate out; sometimes one of them picked up take-out, and sometimes (her favorite) they cooked dinner together sharing a bottle of wine. Weekends were filled with going to Will's family ranch, visiting family, going out with friends, and making wedding plans. Sunday dinners were still taking place, but going to church stopped for the most part. It was much more fun to stay in bed late; after all, they were so busy the rest of the week; they needed the rest on Sunday mornings.

It was shortly after moving in with Will that the hiccups in their relationship began popping up, or maybe he had always been this way; she just didn't know it because they had not been living together. Will was gone ... a lot. Living apart she hadn't noticed how much he was gone. He always had to be out of town for work. However, when he was with her, he was his usual charming and loving self, the way he had always been.

Most of the time she successfully pushed those uneasy doubts deep down and continued to believe in their relationship.

And then, after a few months, Emma Grace woke up and barely made it to the bathroom before everything in her came up.

"Are you okay?" Will asked when she returned to bed.

"I think so," she sighed. "Either I ate something that doesn't agree with me, or I have a stomach bug. Better call the hospital and tell them I won't be there." She picked up the phone, dialed the hospital, and went back to sleep.

Chapter 5

As Tom drove the truck and trailer through the ranch gate and pulled up next to the barn, Luke, who had been looking out the front window with unconstrained anticipation, ran out the backdoor and opened the passenger door before Tom could bring the truck to a complete stop.

"I'm sorry about you getting hurt and all, Uncle Alec, but I sure am glad you're here. You gonna stay awhile, right? I hope it's a long time. Me and you can spend a lot of time together. You can tell me all about your rides. You can teach me how to ride bulls, and I'll do all your chores for you."

"Stop it, Luke," a bit too loud, grumbled Alec's dad as he ambled up to the truck.

"Slow down, Luke, there'll be plenty of time for all of that. Good to see you too, Dad," replied Alec as he slowly lifted his leg and the rest of himself out of the truck and crutched his way back towards the trailer to let Maggie out and put her in a stall.

Tom was already leading Maggie out of the trailer, and Alec whispered to him, "Told you."

"Give it some time and don't start anything," was Tom's whispered reply. "Luke, get your uncle's things and put them in his room."

"Luke, the bunkhouse. I think the bunkhouse will suit me better," and Alec gave Luke a wink.

"Told you you would amount to nothing and be back," was all

Alec's father said as he turned his back on them and strolled back to the house.

"I guess he is going to always blame you for mom dying giving birth to you. I'm sorry, Alec," Tom interjected.

"It's more than that," said Alec as he watched his father walk in the house and let the screen door slam shut. "Let's get Maggie settled and fed and see what Luke's done with my things. "At least someone's glad I'm here."

Alec spent the last days of summer and the first days of fall at the ranch, healing and learning how to lessen the appearance of a limp when he walked. He spent a lot of time doing what chores he could, riding Maggie, and avoiding his father.

During one of the many "riding the fence line" days with Luke, the two of them rode up on Destruction, the bull Alec's father had bought and brought to the ranch for added flavor.

"What do you think about me riding that bull?" Luke asked his uncle.

"Not too keen on the idea right now," was the quick reply.

"Why not?"

"Because you're too young, and I can't teach you right now."

"Destruction's so old, he won't be that hard. You rode him."

"I tried to ride him, and I paid dearly for it. Don't let his age fool you. He's still a wild bull and that makes him dangerous. Stay away from him. I will teach you some day. I promise."

"You always say that, but you don't."

"I will. Trust me," but Luke had already ridden off back to the barn.

A few weeks later, after a typical day of hard work at the ranch for Tom and Alec while Tom's kids were at school, Luke didn't show up for supper.

"Where's Luke?" Tom threw out to anyone at the table.

When no one answered and Tom's quizzical face turned and landed on Wyatt, Wyatt shifted uncomfortably in his chair and answered, "I don't know. I thought he stayed home from school today."

"Why did you think that?" Tom anxiously asked, his eyes fixed on Wyatt.

"Because he didn't get on the bus this morning."

"What?"

"He wasn't on the bus this morning, and he wasn't on the bus this afternoon, so I thought he stayed at home."

After a few anxiously made phone calls, it was confirmed that Luke had never made it to school and no one had seen him all day, not even his closest friends.

Alec said nothing as Tom took a horse, and he took the truck, and the two of them headed for the wide-open spaces of the ranch and the mountains in the distance.

Alec knew if he could just find Destruction, Luke wouldn't be far away.

Finally, off in the distance, Alec spotted the lone bull. But where was Luke? As Alec drove up closer, he saw Luke lying in the pasture. "No," he screamed to himself and sped faster. When the truck came to a break neck stop between Luke and the seemingly complacent bull, Alec jumped out and hobbled over to Luke.

Keeping one eye on the bull he breathlessly asked Luke, "Are you okay?"

"My arm hurts," he said as he tried to keep the tears from showing and the hurt out of his voice.

"Anything else hurt?"

"I don't think so."

"Can you get up and walk?"

"I think so."

"Okay. As quietly and without getting Destruction's attention, slowly walk to the truck," he ordered Luke.

Safely in the truck and headed back for the house leaving the unbothered Destruction behind, Alec's fear was now replaced with anger, and he turned to Luke. "What were you thinking? You could have gotten killed. I told you to leave that bull alone. I told you I'd teach you someday. Why didn't you listen? Not only are you going to be in trouble for skipping school and riding the bull, but you've also gone and gotten me in trouble, too.

Between the soft tears and quiet sobs, Luke offered a genuine but fearful apology, "I'm sorry, Uncle, Alec. I didn't think about that. I hope you won't leave."

There was a long silence between the uncle and nephew, interrupted only by the truck's engine and Luke's quiet sniffling as the truck continued to speed back to the house.

Finally, "Did you ride him?"

"No."

Alec gave a smile to Luke, slapped him on the knee, and told him not to worry about it; he was proud of Luke.

Before Alec could put the truck in park and turn off the ignition, he knew his father was gearing up for another round with him. After many questions and the explanation of where Luke had been and what he had been doing, Alec's father's wrath took full aim at Alec, and just as Alec had predicted, his father blamed him for Luke's uncharacteristic behavior.

There were the same old accusations:

"I'm sure this was your fault."

"Things like this only happen when you're around."

"What were you thinking?"

"What is wrong with you?"

"You never think of anyone but yourself."

"You are completely irresponsible."

"You'll never amount to anything."

But this time his father leveled a new accusation at him, "You are a bad influence on such a young and impressionable kid."

As always, each accusation hit him harder and harder. He was used to the old ones, but this new one of being a bad influence on his nephew was more than Alec could take. His fury boiled over. He dropped his crutches, shuffled over to his father, doubled up his fist,

24

and laid his father flat on his back on the hard ground. His father tried to get up, but Tom held him down while Alec picked up his crutches, got in the truck, and sped off leaving everyone covered in his dust.

Later that evening, Tom found Alec at the nearest bar.

"I thought I'd find you here."

No reply from Alec.

"You know he doesn't mean it," Tom finally said. "He really needs you at the ranch, and so do I, and …"

"Stop," and Alec drained the beer bottle and kicked his stool back. "I don't want to hear it anymore. I'm done." For once, there was no more fight left in Alec.

"Come on; come back to the ranch with me. Tomorrow …"

"I'm going back to the ranch, but only to load up Maggie and leave."

"What about Luke? You know how upset he'll be. You need to at least tell him goodbye."

"I don't care," and Alec left.

Tom followed Alec home and silently watched him as he quietly gathered up his gear, hooked the trailer up to the truck, loaded Maggie into the trailer, and without saying a word to anyone, quietly left the ranch, silently promising himself to never come back. At the end of the ranch road, he stopped the truck and slid out. Holding onto the truck door, he stared back down the road at the dimly lit house in the far-off distance, the pastures bathed in the late night/ early morning moonlight and the dark mountains that loomed in the distance. The only thing greater than the emptiness was the anger inside him that kept his gut on fire. He turned his truck in the direction of the next rodeo and sped off. His father had won; he would not return home to the ranch.

Arriving in Helena, Montana, his first stop was a doctor's office. The cast and crutches were now gone, but not the broken walk.

From this point on he was starting over; no home, no family, no friends, not even Matt and Tom who had stayed behind to work on the ranch. Alec was determined to make it on his own. He gave one hundred percent in preparing for each ride and one hundred percent to every eight second ride. With each rodeo and ride he rose in the rankings. His rides became longer and his scores grew higher. After a few more rodeos, he was back near the top and again a contender for the American Bull Rider of the Year.

Each ride became a short-term release for the deep-seated anger that burned in his soul towards his father and the damage done to his walk. But soon after each ride the anger returned and burned even hotter than before. It manifested itself in Alec's beer drinking and bar fights. Alec convinced himself that he was now homeless and put the full blame on his dad. The more blame he put on his dad, the more his anger burned. The more his anger burned, the more beer he drank. The more beer he drank, the more fights he started. The only release he found for this anger-induced downward spiral was when he was on the back of a wild bucking beast of a bull. Here, his anger merged with the anger of the bull, and the ride became a battle of dominance with anger as the weapon of choice. Even though Alec knew he may have won the battle by laying his dad in the dirt with his fist, he knew his father had won the war by driving him from the ranch. Alec approached each ride telling himself that this ride was not going to be another defeat; this bull was not going to win. He would either be the victor or die in defeat.

December. Las Vegas. Rodeo. Finals. It had been one of Alec's best rodeos to date. The bulls, the rides, the crowds. Alec was a favorite. Whenever the announcer announced, "Alec Wagner up next on … (name of the bull)," the crowd would erupt to a hair-raising roar. They loved him.

But each ride became more difficult than the last. His entire right side seethed with pain, but he had no choice. He had made his decision, so every night he climbed on the back of a wild bull and rode for what seemed like a lifetime. He never heard the crowd; he only heard the bull's snorts, the gate flinging open, the ringing of the bell beneath the bull's belly, and the buzzer indicating that the forever eight second ride was over. He didn't feel the love of the crowds; he only felt the tremendous weight of an untamed tough and mighty beast beneath him jarring his body in a dozen different directions in each hour-long second of an eternal eight second ride. He didn't think about the crowds; he only thought about the next unplanned move of the bull and how to prepare his body so that he wouldn't end up on the ground.

By the last night of the Las Vegas Championship Rodeo, Alec had for the second time, earned enough points and money to be the American Bull Rider of the Year, and as he hobbled out to the middle of the arena to accept his championship belt buckle, he heard for the first time in a long time the applauding roar of the crowd. It sounded good; it felt good. All the pain, all the fights, all the anger, all the setbacks finally paid off. He could smile. He had won. He slowly made his way back behind the chutes and there waiting for him was Scarlett.

Maybe it was the loneliness. Maybe it was the need to celebrate. Maybe he was just tired of fighting. Whatever the reason, he left the arena, and he and Scarlett celebrated The American Bull Rider of the Year for the second time.

The hazy morning after the drunken celebratory night, Tom called. Alec slowly, sleepily, somewhat soberly answered the phone and barely grasped Tom's words, "Dad had a stroke last night. It doesn't look good. The doctors don't give him much of a chance. You might want to come home," were all that registered with Alec's half-working mind.

"Oh," was all Alec said into the phone. Inside he was confused. He had spent so much time hating his father and being so angry with him, but he didn't want this. He didn't want his father to die, but he had also promised himself he would never go back home.

After a long silence in which Tom waited for more from Alec, he finally replied, "We....I....need you back here at the ranch.

Silence again on the phone while Alec sobered up more quickly than he wanted. After the forever silence on the phone, "All right, was his answer.

Chapter 6

I t was close to Christmas, and Emma Grace was in the attic moving boxes and looking for Christmas decorations. She came across an old box and judging by the name on the outside of it, it had been used at one time to carry bottles of liquor. Even though it was wrapped, sealed with duct tape, and not labeled, she cut the tape anyway wondering if this box contained Christmas decorations. On the top was the birthday card she had given Will for his birthday. It was one she had made herself thinking it would mean more to Will than just a store-bought card. On the front of the white construction paper were two half hearts merging into one with handwritten letters saying "Happy Birthday to my other half."

Will had smiled one of his smiles that always melted her heart and said he loved it and that it meant more to him than anything else.

Emma Grace's heart smiled as another soft smile crossed her face. It made her happy to think this was a special box that contained special mementos of their life together. Will had kept the card. What else had he kept that was special to him?

Maybe she should stop and not go through what was evidently so private and personal to him, but this was about their life together, and they shared everything. Her knowing what was special to him would make their relationship even more intimate. So, she kept going.

As she dug deeper through the box of what she believed was

the story of their love, a sickening feeling of confusion and disbelief started creeping over her like a small dark wind that slowly began to drift across her sunlight.

Here was a picture of another woman from years ago, before Emma Grace. She was beautiful with short blonde hair cut in a bob with bangs, lots of make-up, a well-endowed chest, and a large smile. On the back were the words, "I love you with all my heart forever. Molly."

"Okay," she told herself. "Molly was before he knew me, but why would he keep her picture which she had given him with all her heart and love?"

Next, a card. A birthday card from this year. It was addressed to "My best friend, lover, and coolest of the cool." It wasn't signed.

Emma Grace said out loud to herself, "This year? This wasn't from me. Who was it from?"

This obviously wasn't a box of cherished treasures from their relationship. This was more like a collection of treasures from all of his relationships. Was she just another relationship? Something to be added to his collection? The dark wind grew stronger and stronger. There were other souvenirs (Is that what he called this collection of life-changing objects?) of past relationships, but they didn't compare to what she found inside a smaller gray duct-taped box inside the larger gray duct-taped box.

This smaller box contained letters and cards ... and pictures from someone named Lisa.

"The Lisa? The agent at the other end of the prisoner exchanges?" she asked herself.

The life of a boy, Kevin, was laid out in pictures. From his first newborn picture taken eight years ago, to his first birthday picture, to his first day of kindergarten picture, and numerous other birthday and Christmas pictures. The last picture was a picture of him about eight years old standing by a lake this past summer. On the back of the picture were the words, "Camping. Wish you were here. Miss you and love you. Kevin sends his daddy hugs and kisses and misses you." This dark and strong wind had now grown into a tornado that destroyed everything in its past and the present and her future. In one short afternoon with the discovery of the box wrapped in gray duct tape, all of Emma Grace's doubts, questions, fears, and confusion were answered. But the pain, the hurt, the realization of the lie she was living in. ....How does she recover from this?

Emma Grace didn't know how long she lay on the attic floor sobbing from the betrayal, the hurt, the deception, and the loss. When she finally stood up, she knew the relationship was over. What to do next? And somewhere in the back of her mind she remembered something from one of her too distant Bible studies; when the rug is jerked out from underneath you and you land face down, the only thing to do is to come to your knees and turn your face up. On her knees with her face turned toward Heaven, she could find her answer.

And it all became so clear to her now. She had allowed her relationship with Will to become a fortress in her life that defeated anything that tried to encroach into their lives, including her relationship with God. She knew if she confronted Will face-to-face, he would try to explain it all away. He was a master at that, and she was still too weak to fight him. She picked up the phone and called Liz. This would require careful planning, secrecy, and dependence on God with Liz's help. She would also have to wait until Will was out of town on one of his "prisoner exchange trips."

A few weeks later Emma Grace took one last walk through the house to make sure she hadn't left anything behind, the sadness for what could have been overflowed from the emotional well deep down in her gut and slowly crept through every cell in her body until it reached her usually sparkling green eyes and spilled down her drained and tired face. The urge to cry was defeated by the fact that she had no more tears left. The time to move on was way past due. She took one last look at the now empty living room except for his mother's high-back rocking chair, which was now upholstered in the fabric she had picked out, and the sentimental possession of the one remaining belonging of his grandfather's, the one hundred plus year old mantle clock that still chimed every hour.

Laid out in the middle of the floor was the cut-up gray duct tape along with the empty box and all of its contents scattered around. Front and center in the middle of all the scatterings was the smaller box and all of its life-shattering contents. The minute his eyes would fall on that, Will would understand why the house was now empty and why she was gone. She knew he would try to explain away the boxes and their contents:

It wasn't what she was thinking. He loved her and only her. He loved her with every cell in his body. He loved her with all his heart. He loved her best. He was sorry.

She had heard it all before just as she knew his tears would come and his mouth would draw up indicating an ugly cry was coming. He would softly run his hand back and forth across her back between her shoulders, and he would take her hand. She couldn't count how many times he had done that, and each time she was amazed at how her hand disappeared in his. But not this time; she would not give him the chance. She would not believe his "I love you's" and his "I'm sorrys" even though she knew he believed them. She could not take the chance of hearing it again and risk believing it.

Liz stood at the door and said matter -of- factly, "Let's go."

"Wait a minute. One more thing." Emma Grace took off her engagement ring and carefully laid it on top of the smaller box and quickly turned her attention to the almost empty living room. She took her last deep breath of the house, listened for sounds of the past, looked around the now barren living room one last time, whispered goodbye under her breath to the past year of her life, and placed all the smells, sounds, and sights into her memory.

All of her things, except for a suitcase containing a small box of memories tucked inside it and her spiral-kept prayer journal, had either been sold or given to friends. Her parents had just passed away and there was really no other family other than her Uncle Jack to give her things to.

"Why haven't I always kept a prayer journal?" she asked herself. "Maybe if I had always kept one and had kept my close relationship with God, I wouldn't be in this mess."

Everything from this point on was new: new town, new friends, new home, new job; nothing but memories to remind her of this life.

"Don't look back," Liz said. "You're doing the right thing."

"I know," Emma Grace sighed, "Still so sad and so painful."

As Liz reversed the car down the driveway, turned right at the end of the street, and headed towards Emma Grace's new life in Wyoming, Emma Grace knew beyond a shadow of a doubt that this move was the right decision for her, but she wished that her mom and dad were still alive to support her and give her a safe place to land.

She thought of her parents and how much she missed them. She wondered what they would think of her decision to leave Will. She knew her mother would be ecstatic and maybe even her dad. She hated to admit it, but her mother was right; moving in with Will was by far the biggest mistake she had ever made. She had fallen in love with him. She had believed him. She had believed in him. She trusted him. She made the decision to spend the rest of her life with him. All of those commitments to Will she had made without ever praying or seeking God's will, and it was something she didn't think she could ever forgive herself for. She had allowed Will to come between her and her mother, between her and God, and most importantly had cost a life.

"Heavenly Father," she silently prayed, "Forgive me for not listening to you and for being stubborn enough to follow my own wishes and desires. Grant me courage and wisdom to leave the path I was on and start on the new path you have laid out for me. Help me to remember Joshua 1:7 - *Only be strong and very courageous; be careful to do according to all the law which Moses My servant, commanded you; do not turn from it to the right or to the left, so that you may have success wherever you go.* In Jesus's name I pray, Amen."

I can stay another day or so if you need me to," Liz said as she and Emma Grace settled at opposite ends of the newly purchased deep couch across from a lit fireplace.

"That would be nice, but I start work tomorrow and you need to get back and start packing for your move," Emma Grace quietly replied with a smile. "I can't thank you enough for sticking with me and helping to rescue me from … you know … everything. You are an angel sent from God." She closed her eyes and took a long slow sip of wine and savored it in her mouth before allowing the tasty warmth to flow down her throat. "But before you go, I want you to share one more moment with me," she said as she got up from the sofa and walked back to the bedroom. She returned with a box.

"What's that?" Liz asked.

"Come here and help me, please."

"What?" Liz's curiosity was growing, and she moved over next to Emma Grace on the soft rug in front of the fireplace.

I want you to help me put everything in the past behind me once and for all," she said as she opened the box.

"I want you to be a witness for me."

"Okay, but I don't know what you're talking about."

Emma Grace reached into the box and began pulling out remnants of her life with Will. Here's a picture of the two of us riding up on Granny Mountain. "I really thought he would commit to a wedding date on that trip," Emma Grace said with a twinge of disappointment in her voice.

Emma Grace's hand disappeared into the box again and brought out a handful of ticket stubs from all the small town rodeos they had gone to.

"And here are the cards he gave me. He signed everyone with "I love you with all my heart forever. I love you best," and Emma Grace gave a sarcastic and evil laugh with an emphasis on "best" and threw them back into the box.

One more thing. And Emma Grace pulled out a photograph of a sonogram and showed it to Liz.

Liz took the picture from Emma Grace and slowly put down her glass of wine.

Emma Grace watched her as an understanding shadow slowly crept over her face and into her questioning eyes that slowly began to reveal an unspeakable truth.

Liz's eyes moved from the picture to Emma Grace.

Emma Grace shivered from an imaginary slightly chilled breeze before speaking, "You remember when I was so sick with what we thought was the flu? Well, it wasn't the flu."

"...Why ...? Why would you do such a thing?"

"Will wasn't ready."

"What a coward."

"I should have left him after that."

"Yes."

"Emma Grace, why didn't you tell me?

"I was ashamed."

"No need to be with me."

"I couldn't even talk to God about it for a long time. How could I share it with you? Eventually, I took it to Him, and I know He forgives me; I just wish I could forgive myself."

She took the picture out of the box, tenderly held it in her hand, and put everything else back in the box. Then, after tying a ribbon around the box, threw it and all of its contents into the fire.

"Forgive me, Lord."

They both sat there for a long time watching the flames slowly consume what was left of Emma Grace's life with Will.

After a while, "Come on, Liz, toast with me. "To my past with Will and the Will-less future. Lord, I give it all to you and ask for your guidance and hand on me for now and the future.

"Now, my prayer," said Liz. "Lord, help Emma Grace to stay on your chosen path for her. Keep her close to you and may she always remember the love and support she has from me."

Chapter 7

It was early spring, and even though Alec had sworn he would never return to the ranch, here he was. The ranch. The loss of the war. His dad, however, was now living at a retirement center in town recovering from the stroke that left his speech slow and on his better days, a somewhat confused mind.

For Alec, this time at the ranch was better than any time he could remember. Without his father there, he fell in love with the ranch all over again and filled his days breeding horses, mending fences, and taking long rides. But then there was Scarlett who kept showing up at the ranch. Everytime she showed up, Alec threw her off the ranch, but one night at a bar she showed up and Alec gave in. He woke up the next morning to a repeat of the same scene that had taken place so many times before, the morning-after after-taste of whiskey, cigarette breath, sickening sweet perfume, and the onslaught of verbal head-splitting abuses. How was he ever going to break the poisonous cycle of Scarlett?

In the hazy morning of a leftover whisky night and the once again throwing Scarlett out of his life, Alec somehow managed to make it back to the ranch sometime after noon where once again everyone was out looking for Luke, and sure enough, he was found on the ground next to Destruction. However, this time a foot, ankle, or leg was broken and there followed a hurried trip to the ER.

The door to the room occupied by Luke, Tom, and Alec opened

and in walked Emma Grace carrying out her duty turn in the emergency room.

"Deja vu," thought Alec to himself. "She looks so familiar. I know I've seen those green eyes before. Who could forget them?" But Alec couldn't bring himself to talk to her. He left that to Tom as he set his eyes on her and tried to remember where he had seen her before.

After going through the usual formalities of the emergency room questions, tests, and procedures carried out by the doctor and nurse, it was determined that Luke had only sprained his ankle, and he was dismissed with a wrapped ankle and the assistance of crutches.

Emma Grace smiled as she led them out the door and pointed to the exit. "Be more careful next time you try to ride that bull. If not, then next time, maybe I"ll see you for a broken leg. Y'all have a good day," and she smiled as her eyes met and held Alec's eyes.

Alec tipped his hat towards her, smiled, and held her eyes in his.

"Deja vu," thought Emma Grace to herself. "I know I've seen him before.

Who could forget those intense blue-gray eyes?"

After the long shift in the ER, tired, feeling lonely, and not remembering where she had seen those blue-gray eyes before, she went home and tried to call Liz, but no answer. For a brief second, she thought about calling her parents.

"I must really be tired," she thought to herself, "Mom and Dad have been gone for almost a year." Thinking of her parents, Emma Grace untucked the memory of the last time she saw her parents. She and Will had gone skiing with them shortly after she had moved in with Will. Skiing had always been a big part of her life. Her parents, especially her dad, loved the mountains and skiing. They went quite often.

She and Will had spent the last few days skiing with her parents, but they had to get back to Houston because her dad had some big oil deal to close. (He always had a big deal to close; thereby, missing a lot of family time.) Emma Grace and Will had stayed behind for a few more days of skiing. This particular day of skiing was one of the most beautiful days she had ever spent skiing. There was a blue, clear sky with not one fluffy cloud to be seen. The weather was cold, but not freezing. The powder was perfect, and she and Will had gone to the top of the mountain where they could see forever. It was like they were standing on top of the world. It all came crashing down around her when she and Will returned to their room and were given the news of the private plane crash. There were no survivors.

A few weeks later, Emma Grace's phone rang. She had just asked the shoe clerk to bring her a size seven-and-a-half gray ostrich pair of cowboy boots. She had been in Casper now for several months and was finally beginning to actually feel like she was home. She caught her breath as the caller ID registered the incoming call as unknown. Slightly shaking, she turned the ringer off and slipped the phone back in her purse. Doing so, she once again bumped into a man that looked vaguely familiar.

"Excuse me, ma'am," he said with a base-deep, raspy, but soft voice.

Something triggered in her and made her catch her breath.

"Oh, excuse me. I'm sorry; not paying any attention," she quickly answered, again somewhat embarrassed as the soft blush color rose to her cheeks, and there was a feeling of familiarity with this stranger.

"The nurse," Alec said to himself, and he noticed the blush rise in her cheeks. He couldn't help but stare at her as he tipped his hat and walked on. Again, he found himself catching his breath as he held those sparkling green eyes in his stare.

Alec sat down with Luke as he tried on a pair of boots; this was his reward for being such a good patient and staying off his sprained ankle till it healed. His eyes followed Emma Grace as she walked to the other side of the shoe department, sat down, and waited for the shoe clerk to bring her the pair of ostrich boots. Who could forget those piercing green eyes and the early evening sun-dipped hair?

"What do you think of these?" Luke asked Alec.

Reluctantly taking his eyes off Emma Grace, he barely glanced at the boots on Luke's feet and replied, "Those are good-looking."

"Do you like these better than those?" he asked, pointing to the two-tone brown ones he had just tried on.

"Ummm, yeah," came the absent-minded reply. Alec was trying to follow Emma Grace with his eyes, but it was hard to concentrate on her when Luke was so busy competing for attention.

Emma Grace sat down and tried on the boots. Yes, they were expensive, and being from Texas, she had several other pairs of cowboy boots, but she liked them, so she contemplated while her phone silently vibrated in her purse. She slipped her hand into her purse to answer it but thought better of it. It continued to silently vibrate as she tried so hard to concentrate on the boots but thoughts of who kept calling her were vying for her attention. Since saying goodbye to her life in Texas and moving to Casper, she had made it a number one rule to not answer any unknown caller calls. There was always the off-chance that Will had found her. There had been other unknown callers off and on throughout the past months but they had never been as persistent like this time.

She walked around the shoe department and stopped and stared at her booted feet in the mirror. "Yes," she said to herself. "These are the ones."

"Those are good-looking."

A startled Emma Grace looked up into those same hypnotizing blue-gray eyes she had stared into before.

"You should get them."

Before she could reply, he gave her a small smile, tipped his hat as he put it on, and walked out the door.

Her heart skipped a beat, and before she could recover, she could feel the vibrations of her phone going off again in her purse.

Back at home and curled up on the sofa, Emma Grace called Liz so far away in Florida.

"Hey girlfriend," came Liz's familiar and comforting greeting on the other end of the phone.

"Hey," she answered trying to mask the worrisomeness she felt from the many unknown caller calls she had received all day,

"What's wrong?" asked Liz.

"Nothing. Just called to say 'hi' and see how Florida's doing."

"Fine. Nothing new going on. How about with you?"

"Not much." A pause ... and then ...

"Someone's been calling me all day. It comes up unknown, and they've called seven times today."

Another pause ...

"Do you think it's Will?"

"I hope not, but I'm afraid it is. It's the same as the other times, but this time it's more persistent. Call after call. Always coming up unknown."

"Did they leave any messages?"

"No."

"Just like always, huh?"

"Yeh."

"Why don't you answer it?"

"And what do I do if it's him?"

"Tell him to leave you alone."

"I wish it were that easy. You know he won't, and I'm not sure I trust myself."

"Emma Grace, how many months has it been? I really don't

think he would have waited this long to get in touch with you. He's moved on, and it's time you do too."

"Hmmm. Maybe.

"Why don't you start dating?"

"Maybe."

"You always say that. Why don't you take some time off and come down to Florida and stay a week or so?"

"Sounds nice, but I haven't been here long enough to start taking time off."

"Well, try."

"Maybe, but I need to go. Time to go to work."

Now that it was early morning and her shift was over at the hospital, her mind went back to the phone calls. She felt a sense of satisfaction knowing she had not allowed herself to check her phone during the night, but now it was something she could not put off.

Holding her breath, she pulled out her phone. What a relief, not one unknown call. Maybe the thought of Will tracking her down and trying to get in touch with her was just her imagination. With renewed strength and relief, she turned her face up to the heavens and voiced a silent prayer of thank you to the Lord, and she let the brightly lit morning light touch her face with just a hint of warmth and a smile lit up her eyes. She even allowed the thought of the cowboy from the shoe store cross her mind. Why did he look and sound so familiar? His gaze on her and his warm voice stirred something in her. Who was he? Would she ever see him again?

Chapter 8

Now that Tom, with the help of Matt, was successfully running the Wagner Ranch and his dad settled at the retirement facility in town, Alec hit the circuit again full-time, and it proved to be another successful year and another successful Rodeo Final in Las Vegas. Alec won The American Bull Rider of the Year again for the third time, but it had been a tough year on the circuit. He was getting older, and his body didn't recover as quickly from the body-jerking bull rides as it had before. Still, he won, and he and his brother, Tom, who had joined him for the Las Vegas Championship Rodeo, were headed back home to Casper. Tom needed to get back to the business of the ranch and to his four children.

They were in a hurry. They got a later start than they planned because Alec had been celebrating his win and had stumbled back to the hotel quite a bit later than was planned. Tom was driving; driving fast, but Alec wasn't worried. He laid his head back against the headrest and closed his eyes. He was exhausted from the rush of so many rides in so few days, the emotional high of winning again, and the adrenaline rush of celebrating.

It was the brakes squealing and Tom's cry that made Alec fling his eyes open just in time to see headlights light up a large mountain that was too close for comfort and feel his body fly through the windshield and become airborne in the cold December mountain air.

Chapter 9

It was just a couple of weeks before Christmas and it was snowing outside. Emma Grace had been living in Casper for almost a year. The unknown caller calls had stopped, and she felt safe and more sure of herself.

The late night eleven to seven shift on the orthopedic floor of the hospital was quiet except for the whispered buzzing around the hospital about an accident outside of town in which there was one fatality and one critically injured. The critically injured was in surgery right now, and the nurses on the third floor were told to get ready for the new patient. The word was that it was the current American Bull Rider of the Year, Alec Wagner.

"Why did that name sound so familiar?" she asked herself. Maybe she had heard that name on the news; she couldn't remember.

All was quiet on the floor; there were only a few patients when Alec arrived early in the morning, unconscious and accompanied by an entourage of men, old and young.

From the beginning, everything about this patient was different. Mr. Wagner's doctor assigned Emma Grace to Mr. Wagner's room; he became her one and only patient; his room became her new station. When she wasn't on duty; he became the sole patient of other nurses. In other words, Alec Wagner had his own team of private nurses.

"I guess being the American Bull Rider of the Year comes with special privileges," Emma Grace thought to herself.

As time moved forward, the interest in The American Bull Rider of the Year dwindled away; all the hullabaloo surrounding him settled down over the next couple of days. Even the press, which had been camped out on the hospital lawn, finally lost interest or another story replaced Alec's story, and they went away. The only visitor left was a guy named Matt. and sometimes Matt's fiance, Ashley.

Emma Grace became Alec's "private nurse" most every night from eleven to seven. She went about her nursing duties as usual but only for this one patient, Mr. Wagner. She grew accustomed to the new routine and even began to like it. It was quiet. Only the radio (brought in by Matt) playing country songs and the sounds of the machines that were monitoring his heart and breathing could be heard. Every now and then she thought she heard him move or moan, and she would check on him. No change; still unconscious.

One night, shortly after Alec became her patient, preparing him for his first sponge bath, she carefully removed his hospital gown and quickly drew her breath at what she saw.

"What is this?" she whispered to herself and the faint lines in her forehead deepened as she looked with horror at his scarred body. Alec's upper body was covered in scars, from the small half-moon scar under his right ear, to the jagged scar on his right shoulder, to the lone thin scar on his right arm, to the small heart-shaped scar under his heart, down to the circular scar underneath his belly button, and when she turned him onto his side, there were even more scars up and down his back. She recognized the surgical scars, but the others she could only guess where they came from ... failed bull rides, knife fights ...?

"Why would anyone do this to himself?" she asked herself in shock and disbelief. Just who was Alec Wagner; why did this name sound so familiar; and why did he hate himself so much?

Before she could wrap her thoughts around what she was seeing on his body and come to some kind of conclusion, a pretty but made-up, hard-looking woman rushed through the door. This woman took one look at Alec's unconscious body hooked up to an

IV and other machines, and screamed, "Oh no, baby." She turned on Emma Grace and loudly asked, "What's wrong with him? Is he going to be okay?"

"Ma'am, you need to leave. There are no visitors allowed in Mr. Wagner's room.

Did you not see the sign?"

"I'm not leaving; he's my fiance."

The breath was knocked out of Emma Grace, and she quickly grabbed the chart. There was no mention of a fiance. The only names listed to call were his dad and Matt. Then in a little larger print, she noticed, 'Do not let Scarlett Dayton, who professes to be his fiance, into the room.' She called security, and once again, Scarlett was unceremoniously kicked out of not only Alec's room, but the hospital also.

The next morning at home, Emma Grace alone with her God added her new patient to her prayer journal.

Chapter 10

Something wasn't quite right. Alec knew this even before he was fully conscious. His body didn't feel right. He couldn't get a deep breath. His chest was heavy. His sluggish, cloudy mind raced in slow motion to explain where he was and what had happened. Had the bull thrown him and then fallen on him? Had Maggie reared back and fallen on him? He couldn't move his leg. It was caught in something. The rope? The bells? His head hurt. There was something on it other than the familiar cowboy hat. What was it? And the smells; no leather, no livestock, no dirt and sweat; just clean nauseating smells. He had smelled these smells before. He couldn't remember where, but he did know it wasn't good. He listened for familiar sounds: the buzzer, the roar of the crowd, the shouts of the rodeo clowns, the snorts of the bull. Nothing; there was only singing coming from a soft female voice. With great difficulty, he forced his eyes half-way open to a dimly lit hospital room. There was a young pretty woman, long hair pulled back in a ponytail like a magnificent horse's mane, wearing hospital scrubs and sitting with her head bent over a small table writing and singing with the radio. Alec laid there fixing his half-open unblinking gaze at her, not making a sound. Who was she and exactly where was he? Was she a nurse, and he was in a hospital? Was she an angel, and he was in heaven? No, definitely not heaven; he didn't believe in that, but she most definitely could be an angel. Too much to think about now; his head hurt. She was beautiful; the music was soothing. Enough for now. Sleep again.

Conscious again. Too bright, even if his eyes were closed. Too loud, even if the voices were whispering. Too many voices. What were they saying? Something about Tom. What was it? He couldn't quite hear even though the loudness was head-splitting. No music. No singing. No girl. No softness. Just hardness. Enough for now. Sleep again.

Conscious again. Still pain. Still too heavy for him to take a deep breath or move anything. Dark. Good. The darkness didn't hurt so much. Quiet ... except for singing. Was it her? He forcefully peeled his eyes open as much as he could and without making a sound watched her and listened to her singing. Peace. Stillness. Softness. Enough for now. Sleep again.

Conscious again. Still pain, but getting better. The brightness, the loudness, the voices again, and he could understand the voices this time. As he listened to them with his eyes shut, everything came back like a tornado ripping his life apart. He remembered the accident, and he knew without asking that his brother was dead. But what about him? Was he dead? Was he dreaming? Was he unconscious? Was he alive? A tear welled up, but no one noticed. No singing. No girl. No softness. Just hardness. Enough for now. Sleep again.

Conscious again, but different. He could move; not much, but he felt lighter, and he could remember. It was dark again; music again; she was quietly singing with the radio again. He willfully forced his eyes open again, and there she was. He silently and half-consciously watched her for a while longer until she stood up, and he quickly closed his soft blue-gray eyes. He didn't know why, but he didn't want her to know he was awake. Maybe he didn't want to wake up. Maybe he didn't want her to stop singing. He wasn't sure. He could feel her soft intoxicating jasmine-scented presence as she stood close to him reading the machines and checking the IV bag. She lightly took his wrist to check his pulse when Alec slowly turned his fingers toward her and weakly squeezed her wrist.

She looked down into those same eyes she had bumped into back in Houston the first time she had met Will and recognition lit up her eyes. She had run into these eyes, this man, and the raspy voice a few times before. They belonged to the man from the doctor's office and the boot store.

"There you are," she said softly. "Welcome back," and she reassuringly smiled at him. "Do you know where you are?"

"H–h–h–hospital," was the stammered whisper.

"Do you know why you're here?"

And Alec shrugged his shoulders.

"There was an accident. You were badly injured, but you will be okay."

He didn't ask about his brother, and she didn't offer any other information.

"Can I get you something? Water? Ice? Pain medication? Do you hurt anywhere?

"No," he mouthed and dropped his arm, closed his eyes, and was back asleep or unconscious again.

She didn't know. She had doctor's orders to report any signs of consciousness. Emma Grace immediately called the doctor and gave him the news of the awakening of Alec Wagner.

By the time Emma Grace left the hospital that morning, Alec's room was full of visitors … his dad, the doctor, Matt, and Matt's fiance, Ashley. They were all there waiting for Alec to wake up again. She wouldn't be there for that. It was the day before Christmas Eve, and she was going back home to Texas to spend Christmas with her Uncle Jack and his family; the only family she had remaining. Still, there was the early Christmas present of Alec's awakening. She would list it as a "thank you and praise" for today in her prayer journal.

Chapter 11

Two days after Christmas Emma Grace walked back into Alec's room. Other than Alec, there was one visitor, Matt.

"Well, it's good to see you awake," Emma Grace said to her patient. "We haven't been properly introduced. I'm Emma Grace, your nurse for the night shift, Mr. Wagner. It's good to see you've joined the land of the living again. You had me worried there for a while."

She was struck by the intensity of his blue-gray eyes. The color of his eyes may have been pale, but there was nothing pale about the way they looked at her. His eyes, like his deep raspy voice, took her breath away. For some reason, this patient had a strong hold on her.

She began to check his vitals and while doing so she introduced herself to Matt.

"Hi. I'm Emma Grace. It seems like I'll be taking care of your friend here for a while. I'm guessing y'all are buddies?"

"Yes ma'am. I'm Matt, and I'm guessing you're not from around here? Someone as pretty as you and the way you say 'y'all' and 'hi' like it was the smoothest whiskey taking a slow and soft slide down your throat wouldn't have escaped mine and Alec's attention."

Alec shot him a "shut-up look."

"A charmer," she replied and smiled at him.

"Yes ma'am," Matt began but was interrupted by a sharp gruff from Alec.

"For God's sake, Matt, shut up and leave her alone. Let her do her job."

Matt turned towards Alec and with a half-cocked smile and wink nodded in Emma Grace's direction.

Alec quickly looked away pretending he didn't see Matt's response.

Now that Alec was conscious she moved her station back to the nurse's desk down the hall and resumed her normal nursing duties on the floor. Alec was still her patient, and she frequently checked on him. He didn't sleep much, neither did he take much pain medication even though she knew his entire body ached with pain. In addition to the dozens of cuts and bruises and the deep contusion on his head, Alec had sustained several breaks again in his right leg. The doctors had already performed two surgeries to put his leg back together with even more rods and screws, but there was nothing else they could do to make his right leg as long as his left; his right leg was always going to be just a bit shorter than his left. The limp he had before the accident was now going to be a permanent and more pronounced part of Alec's life.

Alec wasn't a very good patient. His refusal to cooperate and his anger were manifested in his constant refusal to take any medication and his habit of throwing his pills at the nurses as he would yell out a string of cuss words had resulted in all medication now being given intravenously. And if they hadn't used an over abundance of tape to tape the IV needle to his arm, he would have jerked that out. He was restless, always trying to get out of bed and usually ending up on the floor. He argued with all the nurses except for her. With Emma Grace, he barely said a word.

Finally, one night when there were just a couple of patients on the floor and things were exceptionally slow and quiet; Alec was more than restless. She went into his room more than once and each time found him on the floor where he ended up after unsuccessfully trying to get out of bed. However, the last time she went into his room to pick him up off the floor she was on the receiving end of a long and very loud list of cuss words that had never been aimed at her before, and she was not going to accept it now. That was that; she had had enough.

"That's it," she shouted. "I've had enough of your actions and words. I have never allowed anyone to talk to me like that, and I'm not going to start with you, Mr. Wagner. I have half a mind to restrain you in that bed, and she called a hospital orderly into Alec's room.

In a forceful tone that made both Alec and the orderly shut-up and stare at her in disbelief, she gave the orders, "I'll be back in five minutes, and I expect Mr. Wagner to be bundled up and in a wheelchair when I get back. He's going outside."

"What are you doing?" Alec bellowed at her when she returned. "I can't go outside; I can't even walk. Besides, it's Wyoming. January. Night.

"You're obviously not happy in here, so you can go outside and walk around all you want to, if you think you can. If you fall, you can pick yourself up or stay out there and freeze to death. I'm tired of hauling you and your wounded pride up off the floor. I'm not doing it anymore."

Alec took one look at Emma Grace's determined face, paid attention to the "don't argue with me" tone in her voice and decided to shut his mouth and not argue. Something told him that Emma Grace could be a formidable foe.

He sat silently in the wheelchair while she pushed him past the empty hospital rooms. Other than leaving for surgery, this was the first time he had been out of his hospital room since they had rolled him in unconscious almost a month ago. There were two or three occupied rooms, and he briefly wondered who was in them and if Emma Grace took care of them as she took care of him. The thought quickly left him as they went down the elevator, through the deserted halls, the automatic doors of the emergency room, and into the frigid and clean mountain night air. For the first time since the accident, he felt he could move. He stretched out his arms; he could fill his lungs with the cold, clean, mountain air. He felt free.

Emma Grace pushed the wheelchair a little way down the sidewalk and went back to sit on the bench by the door where she could leave him to himself but also keep her eyes on him. Alone, outside in the stillness of the night, maybe he could find himself again and be at peace. She watched him from a distance; he was quiet and didn't move much, but through all the bundling up, she could see his shoulders begin to drop, his breaths become deeper and slower, and the muscles in his neck and upper back start to relax.

In the stillness of the frigid night, Emma Grace watched her patient and prayed. She felt a strong attachment to this man. Beneath his gruffness, rudeness, and meanness, she sensed he was wrestling with something but was losing the fight as evidenced by his scarred body. What; she didn't know, but she wanted him to stay around long enough for her to find out. So the entry into her prayer journal for that night would be a prayer that God would lead Alec to peace.

It was a frighteningly cold January night in Wyoming and in spite of being bundled up, she was becoming uncomfortably cold. It was time to take her patient back to his room. Walking up behind him, she cleared her throat to softly break the quiet. He turned, looked at her, and gave her a small smile. That smile took her back to the Houston Livestock Show and Rodeo a couple of years ago, and she remembered the effect that smile and that voice had on her. She took him back to his room and together they managed to get him unbundled and back in bed.

Alec's eyes captured hers and in his deep voice she barely heard, "Thanks."

"You're welcome," she said, also barely audible.

51

And so the late night/early morning routine continued. At some point during the night when everything was quiet and still in the hospital, Emma Grace with quite a bit of muscled-struggle would help Alec into a wheelchair, wrap him up warmly and tightly, bundle up herself, and take him outside. Getting out of the hospital room and outside into the frigid, silent, and lonely Wyoming January nights seemed to help Alec more than anything else.

One night Matt was there when she came on duty which was unusual for so late at night. As she walked in, she heard Alec ask Matt about Maggie. Her ears perked up. Maggie was a name she had not heard before. Who was Maggie?

Emma Grace fiddled with the IV, checked Alec's vitals, tidied up his room, and tried to stay busy while eavesdropping on their conversation. Only after she heard Matt talk about Maggie's visits to the vet and what kind of damage the trailer had sustained in the accident did Emma Grace understand Maggie to be a horse, Alec's horse.

Emma Grace had an idea. When Matt left, she followed him.

Several hours later, Emma Grace bundled up Alec and took him outside just like any other night. This time, however, Maggie was waiting by her trailer in the hospital parking lot. Emma Grace stood back and watched as the horse and owner became reacquainted. She didn't want to interrupt such a moment. Even Matt stood a ways off. There was unspoken communication between Alec and Maggie. Alec couldn't get out of the wheelchair, but Maggie knew enough to lower her head almost to Alec's lap so he could stroke the side of Maggie's face and softly rub above her eyes. Emma Grace could see Maggie respond to Alec's soft words and gentle strokes with her quiet snorts and the up and down shaking of her head. The gentleness Alec showed toward Maggie was a side Emma Grace had not witnessed. She took great satisfaction in seeing this side of him. Somehow she knew this side of Alec had existed, and she was grateful for the moment. Another praise in her prayer journal.

Even though the late night/early morning "walks" had begun

with the thought of easing Alec's restlessness, Emma Grace had begun using these walks as a time spent with her God. It was undoubtedly freezing cold, but it was also peacefully still and freeing. She felt free to see, hear, and feel her God without the interruptions daily life brought. She could see God in the clear moonlight and the never-ending sky blanketed with an eternal number of stars that winked at her. She could hear God in the perfect quietness interrupted only occasionally by a lone wolf far-off in the empty distance. She could feel God in the peace Alec seemed to feel outside in the night air. She knew God was here in this uninterrupted stillness, and she prayed and listened.

These talks with God in these quiet moments usually ended up with her praises for the beauty of the moments and for direction and guidance in her relationship (if one wanted to call it that) with Alec.

She admitted to herself that she liked Alec a lot even though she hardly knew him and didn't understand at all what she did know about him. There was definitely a quietness about him, but there was also a restlessness about him. Judging by his reputation as a bull rider, there was a drive for perfection, but judging by his scarred body, there was also a drive for self-destruction. He was definitely a complicated man, but she loved his deep and gentle voice and the way he looked at her with his intense blue-gray eyes. Emma Grace couldn't explain it, but these walks with Alec and these moments with God not only felt right, but left her with a peace she had not known.

Chapter 12

"**I** should have left for the hospital a lot sooner or called in," Emma Grace announced when she finally arrived at the nurse's station an hour later from when her shift started. "The snow storm has stopped almost all traffic, and I had to walk part of the way to just get here. Sorry I'm late."

"Thank goodness, you're finally here," greeted her from the head nurse. "Alec is uncooperative again. Check his chart and see if there is something we can give him to calm him."

"Sure," and the question of 'What happened to cause him to be difficult again?' popped up in Emma Grace's mind.

"I didn't think you were coming," was the gruff response she received from Alec when she entered his room and saw him trying to push his bed to the window.

"Good evening to you, too," Emma Grace replied, "And what are you doing?"

"Well, if I can't go outside and enjoy the storm, I want to watch it.

"Okay. Fine. Sit down in that chair, and let me move the bed."

She moved his bed in front of the window, opened the blinds, and turned off the lights so he could better see the snow storm.

"There. Get back in bed, and I'll be back in a bit." She knew going outside tonight was out of the question, but maybe watching the peaceful snow storm from the darkness of his hospital room would help him relax and go to sleep.

Hoping he was asleep, she checked on him again in the early hours of the morning, but instead she found him awake, but quiet.

"I thought you were coming right back," he said.

"Sorry. I had some other work to do. Why don't you go to sleep. It's late."

"I'm not sleepy, but if you have a minute, why don't you join me in watching the storm?"

Somewhat startled and thinking for a minute, she agreed and pulled the big chair next to his bed facing the window. They sat there awkwardly quiet and watched the wind-driven silent snow fall blanketing Casper.

"How did you come to end up in Casper?" he suddenly asked, breaking the silence.

She jumped a little. What a surprise he was. He hardly ever spoke to her, and now he was asking a personal question.

"It's okay," she told herself. "He doesn't know you, so he couldn't possibly know that long ugly story you have tried so hard to forget. He's not intruding; he's just trying in his own way to start a conversation."

Since this was the only time he had asked her anything, she decided to go down that road.

"Well, I'm actually from Texas," she said. I lived there my whole life until almost a year ago. I was in a relationship that didn't work out." A long pause …

"How much should I tell?" she asked herself and then decided to continue. "It's not that I was ever afraid for my life, physically, but I had to end it and get away. I came here because I didn't think he would find me here."

"Has he?" Alec asked after realizing she wasn't going to elaborate.

"No," she answered louder than she needed.

The uncharacteristically talkative and inquisitive Alec continued, "What about the rest of your family?"

For unknown reasons to herself, Emma Grace decided to expose this wound to Alec even though she hadn't visited it in a while, so she proceeded.

"My parents died in a plane crash last year, and I never had any brothers or sisters. I have an uncle and his family that I'm somewhat close to. He looks after my finances and makes sure that I"m doing okay, but that's all."

A silence filled the room broken only by the low music in the background and the unspoken thoughts of Alec and Emma Grace.

Finally, "Enough about me and my dull life. Tell me about you. Why do you do what you do?"

"You mean why do I ride bulls?"

"Yeh. Why do you do that to your body?

There was a stillness and a peace as their eyes locked, and then Alec moved his stare from her eyes to the raging snow storm outside the window while he thought about her questions. There was silence, and she watched him as he seemed to drift back to another place and time. The here and now left his gaze as he reflected back to his first attempt at riding a bull.

After a hesitation, he began. "One day when I was about fourteen me, Tom, and Matt were just goofing around at the ranch when the three of us dared each other to get on Destruction, a bull at the ranch, and see which one could stay on him the longest.

Tom, being the oldest, tried first but went flying through the air before his body made full contact with Destruction's back. Matt was next, and he quickly found himself flying through the air but not before his body was jerked around in a million different directions. Next was my turn. Tom and Matt tried to talk me out of it. I guess they were scared for me."

'It's not worth it. Don't do it,' they pleaded with me.

"Of course, after that, I was for sure going to ride him. I may have been younger and definitely smaller, but I wasn't going to let them get something over on me. So, I tried to learn from their mistakes. I stood very still. I don't think I even breathed. I just kept my eyes on Destruction's fear-filled but ready-to-fight eyes and slowly, patiently and deliberately walked towards him, reducing the size of the circle with each determined cautious step. It became a contest of who would blink first, look away, and walk away. When I circled around towards the bull's back-end, Destruction circled his body, also not taking his wild eyes off me. I kept circling him until he grew bored, took his eyes off me, shook his head, and snorted. That's when I saw my chance and quickly jumped on his back.

I didn't know my body could move in so many directions at one time, and before I knew it, I was in the air, on the ground, and running for the fence. I made it and climbed over. As soon as I caught my breath, I knew I was going to ride Destruction or die trying.

I've been riding bulls ever since that day over twenty years ago, and now here I am, a walking testament to what bulls can do to a body, sitting in a hospital room talking to a pretty nurse I don't know very well, and will in all likelihood never professionally ride again."

Alec took his eyes off the snow storm outside and set them back on Emma Grace giving her a small smile.

"Thank you for the compliment."

Another silent pause as a bewildered Emma Grace looked questioningly at him, and he kept his eyes locked on hers.

"What do you think you'll do?" she finally asked.

"I don't know," was the hesitant answer. I guess I'll go back to the ranch and heal. After I'm healed, I'll probably try riding again."

"Why? Why would you risk it?

"I don't know anything else. Besides, it irritates my father and that gives me some satisfaction. We've ... he and I ... have never liked each other much."

"How sad," replied Emma Grace, searching Alec's eyes and face for a comeback.

There wasn't one.

"How do you like Casper?" he all of a sudden asked.

She looked back out at the snowstorm realizing he wasn't going to comment on her comment.

"I actually like it a lot."

"Good."

She felt his gaze on her; she turned and smiled at him. He smiled back, and she replied, "I'm glad you shared your story with me."

Chapter 13

Alec began to look forward to the nightly "walks" with Emma Grace more and more. He tried not to show it, but he counted the hours till seven o'clock when she showed up for her shift. He admitted to himself that she affected him; she affected him in a way that made him excited and uneasy at the same time. She was pretty, gentle, and strong. Those first nights after the accident it was Emma Grace that kept him alive; it was she and her singing that gave him a reason to wake up. Her jasmine-scented presence of comfort and peace accompanied by her beautiful soft singing were the reasons he had kept opening his eyes. Although most of their shared experiences had been spent mostly in silence, Alec knew he liked her, probably even more than he wanted to admit to himself. That made him very uneasy, He didn't want to be committed to one person. He wasn't dependent on anyone, and no one was dependent on him. He was like one of the untamed bulls he rode; free and independent.

The next morning Alec's ailing father showed up in his room with a lawyer. They stayed for most of the morning and were still there when the doctor walked in.

"Good news," he said. "I believe you are well enough to go home tomorrow provided you keep up your physical therapy everyday. Besides, there isn't much else we can do for now."

Alec looked at the doctor, perplexed, "But I can hardly walk. I don't want to leave here until I can walk on my own without crutches."

"Alec, this is the best I can do. You'll lose the crutches in time. You've got to give yourself time and more physical therapy, but you can do that at home. Once again, you're lucky you get to keep that leg. And I don't recommend professional riding anymore. Your head contusion was serious enough that another head injury could permanently paralyze you or even kill you."

The same thing he had heard before.

Between the news his father and the lawyer had brought him and now the doctor's news, Alec briefly wished he had died along with his brother in the car accident.

Emma Grace walked onto the hospital's orthopedic floor looking forward to seeing Alec. Without her actually acknowledging it, Alec had become an important part of her world. She sat down at her station and opened up Alec's chart to check on his day: progress on his physical therapy, his diet for the day, his vitals, and any new doctor's orders. She looked at the doctor's new orders with disbelief. Alec was being discharged tomorrow. The thought had never even entered her mind. Of course, she was a nurse and the goal was to treat the patient until they were well enough to go home, but she didn't want Alec to go. She had been so engrossed in her world of nightly "walks" with him that the thought of him not being there didn't exist. The doctor's new order jolted her back to reality. How in the world was she going to be able to walk into his room and pretend that she was happy and excited that he was able to go home? Above everything else, he was her patient, and he could never be anything more than that. What was wrong with her? How could she have let her feelings get the best of her? She knew she was going to have to walk into his room at some point, but she put it off as long as she could.

She finally walked into his room that night half expecting him to ask her why she was late; she didn't know how she would answer, but she knew she had to be professional.

She decidedly put on a smile and tried to sound happy and excited for him.

He was up, sitting in the big chair staring out the window. His back was to the door and her. He did not turn around when she entered the room and greeted him.

"Hi," she said. "Well, it looks like you are feeling better. So good that you get to go home." She wasn't sure if he could detect the disappointment in her voice, and she didn't know if she wanted him to know what she was feeling or not.

"Yes," he replied. His voice was flat and unemotional.

She walked over to him so she could see his face. It was blank; she thought she spied a little bit of anger in it. Their eyes met and she sensed a moment of understanding and hope; then it was gone in the same instant it appeared.

"Can I get you anything? Can I help you back in bed?" she asked.

"No. Leave me here," was the reply, quiet but harsh.

"Mr. Wagner, I really need to check your vitals."

"I'm good. Come back later," and then, "please."

"Ok," she quietly said and left. A lump rose up in her throat, and she fought it back down along with the tears.

She tried to stay out of his room as much as possible. It hurt. She had known hurt before and had no desire to return to it. This was her fault; she knew not to get emotionally involved with a patient. Not many conversations had even taken place between them and certainly no feelings of affection/attraction had been played out or even spoken about. She felt they had shared a lot and had achieved a mutual understanding and respect for each other through their nightly excursions outside. She felt she had broken through his tough hide, so what happened? Tonight he was as cold as the February Wyoming night.

She finally found her composure and went in to ask him if he wanted to go for a walk one last time. To her surprise, she found him bundled up and ready to go.

"I didn't know if you wanted to go tonight," she said, hiding her surprise.

"One last time," he said. "Only this time I'm walking … with the help of these," and he lifted up one of his crutches.

"Okay. Let me get my coat," and as she walked out, the lump and tears came back at the words, "One last time." Again, she fought them back down.

They rode the elevator down to the first floor, walked through the halls and out through the emergency room. It was strange having Alec walking beside her and holding doors open for her.

Tonight, they sat on the bench together. It was cold and silent. Far off they heard the coyote again. There was so much she wanted to say, but she couldn't, so they sat there in silence. Emma Grace turned her thoughts again to her Lord, comparing this cold and silent winter night to the night long ago when the baby Jesus was born. She imagined it was a night much like this; cold, quiet, still, peaceful, and she appreciated the thoughts. She wanted to remember every moment and write a praise in her prayer journal for the special experience.

She said to herself and to her Lord: "Heavenly Father, help me to remember every moment of this beautiful night. You know my heart and my feelings. I give them to you to use according to your will. Thank you. In Jesus's name. Amen."

Finally Alec turned and set his blue-gray eyes into hers and shyly smiled at her. He took her hand and without any words passing between them, they went back to his hospital room for his last night there.

Before leaving after her shift, she made herself go back to Alec's room and even though it was early morning, he was sitting in the chair looking out the window. One quick glance at the bed told her he had not slept in it at all.

"Hey," she said, surprising him. "Can I talk to you for a minute?"

He rose from the chair, turned towards her, set his intense gaze on her, and offered her the chair.

"No thanks."

A long pause while they stared at each other and tried to read into what was not being said.

Finally ..."I just wanted to tell you before you go home how much I have loved being your nurse and getting to know you. I know you're not happy with the outcome of the accident, but I believe with rehab you'll be back to the old Alec before you know it."

He continued to stare at her so intensely without speaking; it began to make her feel confused. He had that effect on her.

After another pause, she continued forcefully cheerful, "I hope I haven't done anything to upset you because I have enjoyed so much getting to know you. I'm glad for you that you're well enough to go home, but things won't be the same around here. I'll be off duty when you check out, so all the best to you. Come back and visit sometime. I'll miss you and our nightly "walks." Now what excuse am I going to use to get out of this place for a few minutes each night?" She gave him a slightly forced smile and began to walk out.

"Emma Grace, can you wait a minute?" he asked, and she sensed an uncertain almost pleading tone in his voice as he kept his eyes from meeting hers. "I know I've been cold and unfriendly to you tonight, but it's not what you think." Hesitatingly ... "I found out today that my brother's children are going to have to move to Arizona with their mother's family if I can't take them in. I can't take them in, but I also can't let them go to Arizona. Luke and Wyatt may remember their grandparents, but I know Emily and Lily don't. They have never even seen Lily. They washed their hands of Kathy when she became addicted to painkillers after Lily was born. The kids have lost both their parents. I know it's probably hard to believe, but I am close to them, especially the oldest boy, Luke. I don't know what I"m going to do. That's where my mind has been tonight; it didn't have anything to do with you. You have been the best medicine for me. I don't know if I would have survived without your singing and our nightly 'walks.' Thank you for all you've done."

"Well, take them in. There's no reason for you not to. I'm sure it won't be easy. You may have to give up a lot, like riding, but your nieces and nephew need you. You are not that cold-hearted; I know."

"It's not as simple as you make it out to be. I want to take them, but ... (a long pause) ... the will says in order for me to have them ... (another long pause as Alec turned his back to her and the words stuck in his throat) ... I have to be married.

The "I have to be married" words were almost inaudible, and Emma Grace at first wasn't sure she heard correctly.

"I guess my brother didn't think I was responsible enough to take care of my own nieces and nephews. Can't say that I blame him for thinking that. I haven't exactly been someone he or anyone else could count on. I've always been so determined to make it all on my own without help from anyone that I haven't been there for anyone. Now Tom's kids have to pay for my selfishness. I don't know what to do. My selfishness killed Tom and now it's going to destroy the kids' lives. I've been with a lot of women, but I can't marry any of them and expect them to be a mother figure for the kids."

There was a long pause with Alec's back still facing Emma Grace. Then in a quiet, almost inaudible voice, Emma Grace replied, "I'll marry you, Alec."

He awkwardly and slowly turned around to face her and look into her eyes.

"What did you say?" he quietly asked in disbelief, afraid to hear the answer.

"I'll marry you," she said with a gentle smile.

"Why would you do that?"

"I have my reasons."

Alec didn't say "okay," but he didn't say "no" either.

Emma Grace walked over to Alec, gave him a light kiss on his cheek, told him she would be back before he checked out later that morning, and walked out. She went straight to her desk at the nurse's station, gathered her things, gave her final notice to her supervisor, walked out the hospital doors, drove through the quiet streets of Casper, and went home.

Chapter 14

Alec was speechless. He was in disbelief. He didn't actually agree to the marriage, but he knew he would go through with it.

He had never wanted to get married. He had spent his life convincing himself and others he didn't need or want anybody. He loved his freedom, and being a rodeo star and the American Bull Rider of the Year brought a lot of pretty ladies with the territory, but Emma Grace was different. She was beautiful; no one could deny that, but more importantly, she seemed to understand him. She was always near, but never intrusive. She knew what he wanted and what he needed before he did. She had saved his life with just her presence ... and her singing. It was her singing that had caused him to open his eyes.

But why did she want to marry him? He was just an old worn-out, broken-down cowboy who didn't even have two good legs to walk on. They had had very few conversations; in fact, their main way of communicating was through lengthy silences, but there was something unspoken between them. He felt she understood him. She was right about their nightly outings; she was right about leaving him to his thoughts; she was right about Maggie.

What else did he know about Emma Grace? Not much. He had always been consumed with his own misfortune and trying to heal, that he hadn't thought to find out much about her. In fact, there had only been that one conversation the night of the snowstorm. She didn't spill much. What happened in that relationship that made her run away? What was her favorite color? Could she cook? Did she know anything about raising kids? He certainly didn't. Did she even like kids? Would they like her? Did she plan on still working? He began to realize he didn't know her at all. He had just a few short days to get to know her; he forgot to tell her that he had to be married in less than a week before Luke, Wyatt, Emily, and Lily had to leave the only home they had ever known and go live with the grandparents they didn't know.

The words, "I'll marry you," came out smoothly without thought or hesitation. The second she realized what she said was the second she felt a blessing from God. He was answering the prayers and the praises she had given to him on all those nightly walks and in all those quiet moments. Others would be shocked and probably opposed to this, but nothing had ever felt more right and brought more peace to her than anything she had ever known. This fit. This was a God-thing; it was questionable and unexplainable to the world but made perfect sense to her. And she knew, to Alec also.

She left Alec's room, rushed out of the hospital for the last time as an employee, and even though it was not quite daylight decided to call Uncle Jack anyway.

It was mid-morning when she arrived back at the hospital. She knew they wouldn't check out Alec before noon. She also knew his father and Matt would be there to take him home.

"Maybe I should find out where 'home' is," she thought to herself.

Alec suddenly and quietly said, "Wow," to himself when Emma Grace walked back in his room. Prior to this he had only known her as Emma Grace, his nurse, in nurse's scrubs and a ponytail; he didn't know her as Emma Grace, woman, in street clothes with long beautiful hair falling past her shoulders. She looked good in jeans and boots. He was not expecting it, and the realization of "Oh, my god, the pretty lady I bumped into in Houston, the boot store, and the ER with Luke," flooded his face with a bright smile.

Alec gave her a smile, and to his surprise, an uncontrollable wink when she walked in. She smiled and winked back. Without any warning or build-up, Alec announced, "You all know Emma Grace who has taken such good care of me since I've been here? Well, we're getting married Friday."

Shocked at the sudden announcement of Friday as the wedding day, but through a show of sincerity and agreement, Emma Grace walked over to Alec and gave him a kiss on the cheek. He responded likewise. He grabbed her hand, and together they faced a speechless and shocked audience of two.

Then the questions came:

"What?"

"Are you sure?"

"When did this happen?"

"So soon?"

"You're not just doing this for the kids?"

Much to Emma Grace's surprise Alec answered all the questions like he had been prepared for them. Emma Grace and I are getting married on Friday. She has been my nurse for over two months, and believe me, no one knows me better than she. We are getting married for our own reasons."

"Isn't that curious that you are getting married just before time runs out according to Tom's will and the children have to move to Arizona?" was his Dad's only comment.

Alec ignored it while there was an awkward silence, and after the hesitation, the congratulations began. Then one of the assistant hospital administrators walked in, dismissal papers were signed, Alec was wheelchaired out, and Emma Grace drove both of them home.

With Alec giving directions, Emma Grace drove through the busy streets of Casper to the outskirts of town and for the next thirty minutes or so drove through the wild and beautiful countryside of

Wyoming until at last they came to the gate of the Wagner Ranch. Through the gate and up the long dirt road to the house, Emma Grace slowly drove.

She stopped the car and stared at the house before going inside. It was a two-story Victorian that looked like it had been built at the turn of the twentieth century. At one time it had been painted a nice white with dark brown trim. There was a front porch that ran about two-thirds along the front with a large bay window that protruded out at the end of the porch. It had been a beautiful house at one time, but years of neglect made it look sad and in need of many repairs: a new roof, new paint, new steps, and new porch railing.

She grabbed Alec's bag and gingerly followed him as he crutched his way up the front steps and across the porch where Emma Grace was convinced that no one had walked in months, if not years. The front door opened up into a foyer where an old staircase with an intricate wooden carved banister led to the four bedrooms and one bathroom upstairs. To the right of the foyer was the living room that ran all the way to the back. In the front of the living room was the large bay window. On the opposite wall was the much used and ash-filled fireplace with dingy built-ins on either side. Above the built-ins were what once were beautiful stained-glass windows. What colors were the stained-glass, Emma Grace could not tell. At the back of the room was a doorway to the left that led to the kitchen and a back wall of windows that framed the snow-covered mountains in the distance. To the left of the foyer was the never used dining room where windows looked out on the never used front porch. On the opposite wall were even more windows that looked out over the spacious Wyoming countryside. Either through the dining room or at the end of the foyer was the kitchen.

In the kitchen was an old yellow and green faded linoleum patterned floor. In the middle of the faded patterned floor was an old oblong early American maple table with cafe table chairs. There was a harvest green gas range and stove left over from the 1960s or '70's (she wasn't sure) with the matching harvest green dishwasher. There was also a fairly new refrigerator. She knew it was newer because it was stainless steel and not harvest green (Someone had broken up the harvest green kitchen appliance matching set.); however, she was afraid to open it; there was no telling what was inside it or how it smelled. The kitchen sink overlooked a screened-in back porch. Upstairs there were four fairly small bedrooms (two on each side of the stairs) and one large square bathroom at the top of the stairs.

Alec stayed downstairs while Emma Grace went to look upstairs. While she was up there, Alec stood at the living room bay window and looked out at the ranch. He had been coming back to the ranch in between rodeos since his father had suffered the stroke and had moved into assisted living care in town. Their relationship had somewhat improved since the stroke, and Alec felt more at home on the ranch than he could remember. It felt good to be home again and to be a part of the wide-open spaces. He could stretch; he could breathe deeply. He could feel all the pent-up feelings and thoughts ooze out of his body with every breath he took. Yes indeed, it was good to be home, but now he was looking at the house like he had never seen it before.

He knew it was a mess. He knew it was in need of many repairs; it just never seemed important before. When he was home, there had always been more important things to do: feeding, vaccinating, doctoring, breaking, roping, mending fences, but nothing for the house. Emma Grace's presence made the house seem so drab and lifeless.

"I know it looks pretty bad and there's a lot to be done," he said with a hint of an apology as Emma Grace came back downstairs. "I'll get things fixed."

"Okay," was the quick reply, and she handed him her uncle's business card.

"What's this?" he asked.

"That's my uncle's business card. I talked to him this morning, and he's expecting your phone call."

"Why?" As he looked at the card, questions began to appear on his face. "This card says Williams and Williams Oil & Gas, and the name on it is Jack Williams, CEO. Jack Williams of Williams and Williams Oil & Gas is your uncle?" he asked, staring at her with eyebrows raised.

"Yes. And my father was Frank Williams of Williams and Williams, the CEO and co-owner of one of the largest oil and gas companies in the nation that was killed in that private plane crash last year. My uncle took over after dad died."

"You're that Williams?" Alec asked in disbelief.

Emma Grace absentmindedly nodded her head yes.

"Then why are you working as a nurse so far from home in Casper, Wyoming and living all by yourself, away from your family and the business?"

"I told you about my relationship with my old boyfriend Will and having to get as far away from him as possible. I'm the odd duck of the family; I've always gone my own way. I love nursing; it's always given me a purpose. I know you and your family have money, but I don't want you to think I'm marrying you for your money. I have my own. My uncle wants to make sure I'm protected as well as you. So, you should call him."

Alec had no words. And although he didn't really care, he had made up his mind that she was marrying him for his money. It was common knowledge that the American Bull Rider of the Year came from money his family made from the ranch and that the money earned from his winnings was just icing on the cake.

"Alec?" she interrupted his thoughts, and he looked up from the Williams and Williams card and questioningly looked into her eyes. He liked the way his name sounded when she said it; he smiled and his heart rose to his throat.

"I hate to start out this way, but I see only one bathroom. Am I missing the second one?"

"No. We only have one."

"So, all six of us are supposed to use one bathroom?"

"I guess. I haven't thought about it." He was still trying to wrap his mind around the Williams thing.

"I don't think that's going to work. Can we enclose the back porch and build another bathroom?"

Alec, halfway listening, replied, "Yes," while trying to figure out what he was going to say to her uncle, and more importantly, what was her uncle going to say to him

"Hey. Where's the nurse?" Matt asked, walking into the house after taking Mr. Wagner back to the retirement center.

"She's upstairs or in the kitchen trying to figure out where to put another bathroom. And her name is not Nurse; it's Emma Grace."

"What's going on, Alec?"

"What do you mean?"

"You're getting married … to someone you don't know."

"I know her well enough."

"You can't possibly know her well enough. We all know you're doing this for Tom's kids, but have you thought about the money? It's no secret how much money the Wagner's have. I hate to say it, but maybe she's in it for the money."

Alec shot him a "shut-up" look, and Matt retreated somewhat for a minute.

'I mean … hey, I think you're a good guy, but most people don't know you that way. And especially a lady like Emma Grace.

"I'm not letting someone like Scarlett raise Tom's kids. Here," replied Alec, "this is her uncle's business card, and I'm supposed to call him."

Matt looked at the card. His eyes grew large as he looked over at Alec.

"Jack Williams is her uncle?" he shockingly asked.

"Yes, and her father was Frank Williams, the one who died in that plane crash last year."Oh."

"I know," said Alec.

Chapter 15

T he biggest and most pressing problem that needed immediate
attention was the kids, Tom's kids; they were the ones responsible
for the hasty marriage of these two people from such different walks
of life, had nothing in common, and who barely knew each other.
Emma Grace had never seen, much less met these four children
from ages seven to thirteen. If it hadn't been for her faith in that
she was doing the right thing, she would never have agreed to be a
substitute mother to a child, much less to four children, much less
to children she had never met, much less to children who had been
mostly raised by only a father. The thought of being a mother to
these four unknown children and marrying a man whom she barely
knew scared her to death, but she had her faith.

One afternoon after Alec's visit to the physical therapist, Emma
Grace and Alec stopped by the kids' schools and picked them up.
First stop was Luke at the middle school.

Luke's face, which was always an open book, turned from
excitement to see his uncle picking him up from school, to a frown
when he saw a woman in the car. "Who's she?" Luke growled,
showing his disappointment that someone else was in the car besides
his uncle and giving Emma Grace a stare-down.

"Luke, this is Emma Grace. She was my nurse in the hospital
and she drives me to and from physical therapy," was Alec's answer
to Luke's growl. "Let's be nice."

"Hi, Luke," came the pleasant greeting from Emma Grace as she turned to greet Luke who plopped down in the backseat. A question flashed across her face as to why Alec introduced her as his nurse and not as his fiance.

"Think about it later," she said to herself.

No reply to her greeting came from the tall but skinny soon to be thirteen year old seventh grader, but he was full of talk for his uncle.

After Luke, came the elementary school stop for the rest of the brood. Wyatt, a stocky, awkward eleven year old in fifth grade was added next to the backseat, but didn't have much to say during the ride home. The nine year old third grader, Emily, like her brother, Wyatt, didn't have much to say but the jeans and cowgirl boots gave away her interest in anything having to do with horses. Then there was Lily, (Emma Grace's favorite, even though she knew she wasn't supposed to have favorites), a tiny, blonde-haired little girl dressed from head to toe in pink, a pink dress, pink tights, pink boots, and a pink coat, and who enthusiastically greeted Emma Grace. Lily was full of questions for Emma Grace.

"Who are you?"

"How do you know Uncle Alec"

"Are you still his nurse even if he isn't in the hospital anymore?"

"I got a hundred on my spelling test, but I failed my math test."

"Do you want to see my drawing I did in school today?

Emma Grace did her best to smile and answer all of Lily's questions, but the competition with Luke's conversation with Alec and not really knowing what to tell Lily about the nature of her relationship with Alec soon became overwhelming.

"Oh my goodness," thought Emma Grace. "What have I taken on? I don't know if I can do this. Four of them are so many. Is it too late to back out?" She silently turned to God and prayed quickly as the questions kept coming from Lily. "Help me, Lord. Thank you. In Jesus's name. Amen." She turned back to the backseat, smiled at Lily and patiently waited for the next question.

The next stop was their grandfather's cottage at the retirement center to pick up their clothes. Even though life for the children had been stable while they were living with their grandfather, it had not been home, and now they were moving back to the ranch where they had not been since their father died. They were anxious to get back to their beds, their rooms, and all their pets at the ranch. Too many changes had come quite frequently to the short lives of Tom's kids with their mother abandoning them, their grandfather's stroke, the comings and goings of their dad and uncle with the rodeo business, and finally the recent life-changing death of their dad. They were never quite sure who would be at the house when they got off the bus after school. Emma Grace somewhat understood this and tried to remember how much their lives had changed, and she believed that the one thing they needed the most was stability accompanied with lots of unconditional love.

Emma Grace woke up early on her last day in her townhouse. It wasn't exactly how she had dreamed her wedding day would be like. She had always thought that she would be surrounded by her friends, her bridesmaids, the hairdresser, the make-up artist, the photographer, lots of flowers, and a beautiful long white dress. She had dreamed there would be lots of laughter, happiness, jokes, teasing. But, the reality of this day, her wedding day, was dressing by herself in an ivory dress she ordered online at the last minute. Instead of a church filled with all of her friends and family, there was only she, Alec, Matt, Ashley, and the preacher in attendance. Instead of a church covered in white roses and lilies, there was only her bouquet of white roses. There was a short wedding ceremony at the First Baptist Church of Casper where Emma Grace was a member; she insisted that they marry in a church. Alec didn't belong to a church.

His only comment on getting married in a church was, "Okay, but just know that I probably haven't stepped foot in a church more than a dozen times. And that was only for funerals and weddings. Don't expect to make me a church-goer." There was a nice lunch with Matt and Ashley, Matt's fiance, to celebrate the unexpected nuptials and then Alec and Emma Grace picked up the kids from school and went home.

The first night together as a family in the house was awkward. As soon as they got home, the kids scattered to their rooms and outside to the barn and their pets. Alec claimed the stairs were still a little difficult for him to manage, so he thought it best for him to sleep on the sofa downstairs. Emma Grace made the sofa for him as comfortable as she could, gave him an awkward nervous smile, said goodnight, and retreated upstairs to the master bedroom which was now her room. After a long hot bath, she checked in on the kids who were all asleep, except for Luke who was still playing games on the TV in his room, and crawled into bed. She gave herself into the tears that she had held back for so long. So much had happened so fast. Was she doing the right thing? Yes, she still believed she was, but this was not how she had pictured her wedding night. Although she knew sex with Alec was out of the question for now because of his injuries, she had hoped they could at least share a bed. Did he really dislike her so much? She was very much aware of his playboy reputation and his past relationship with Scarlett, and according to Scarlett, there was still a relationship between her and Alec.

A prayer and entry into her prayer journal: "Heavenly Father, here I am again coming into your presence on bent knees, bowed head, and repentant heart. I know you've led me to this point, and you won't desert me now. I'm scared, but my trust in you is greater than my fear. Grant me your wisdom and guidance. Thank you for today and for this family. Protect this family, my family. Bless us and help us to love and support each other. I claim your promise in Jeremiah 29:11: *For I know the plans that I have for you, declares the Lord, plans for welfare and not for calamity to give you a future and a hope.* Thank you. In Jesus's name, Amen."

Emma Grace felt better. The tears subsided. Peace flooded her. Sleep settled in.

Should he have at least given her a light kiss on the cheek? After all, they were married and this was their wedding night, ... but the circumstances for them were so different. He had never known a lady like her; well, maybe Ashley, but she was more like a sister. Emma Grace was definitely no Scarlett, and he found himself in awe of her, of her softness, of the way she smelled like fresh jasmine, of her sorrel-colored hair touched by the sun, of the gentle smile, of her long and slightly curved body, and of her soft southern-accented voice. He knew he didn't deserve her, and he feared she would soon discover that and leave. So, best for now not to get too close to her and not let her get too close to him; the less she knew about him, the better. Sleep did not come easily for Alec on his first night home.

He woke up to the smell of coffee and bacon frying the next morning. Curious, he walked into the kitchen where he found Emma Grace cooking breakfast.

"What are you doing?" he asked, not hiding his surprise.

'"Good morning," was the pleasant answer with a smile. "I'm cooking breakfast.

Did you sleep well?"

"Yeh, but we don't usually eat breakfast this early on a Saturday morning, and then it's usually just cereal," Alec replied.

"That's ok," Emma Grace answered back. "I'm making pancakes. I'll just save the batter until the kids wake up. Do you want some pancakes?"

"Yeh. Sure," and Alec helped himself to a cup of coffee.

The two of them sat down in the deafening noiseless warm-smelling kitchen and ate breakfast. Alec didn't know what to say, so while avoiding eye contact with her, he busied himself eating his breakfast in a hurry saying he needed to get out to the office in the barn. Besides, he didn't know what to say to Emma Grace. Even though she was his wife, they had barely had one conversation. What would he say? What are your plans for the day? Is there anything you need? What can I do for you? Why did you marry me? How long is it going to take you to realize you've made a mistake and leave? He decided not to ask any questions; he didn't want to know the answers.

Before they finished, still half asleep Lily walked in with tousled hair. She looked around to see what there was to eat.

"Good morning," was Emma Grace's pleasant greeting.

With no reply or acknowledgement, Lily sat down, looked at the leftover syrup-covered plates and asked for some pancakes. Emma Grace promptly poured the pancake batter into two silver-dollar sized pancakes onto the skillet and offered Lily some bacon along with juice.

Emma Grace and Alec both sat in silence and watched Lily devour her pancakes, bacon, and juice, and then ask for more. While she consumed her second helping of pancakes, Wyatt walked in loudly asking what smelled so good. After the cordial good morning and making of some more silver-dollar pancakes, Emma Grace and Alec silently watched as the same scene repeated itself with Wyatt.

In the quiet consumption of breakfast, Wyatt was the first to speak, :Why can't we have breakfast like this all the time?"

"I didn't know that's what you wanted," was Alec's delayed reply.

"Sure. I love pancakes."

Walking through that open door, Emma Grace cautiously asked, "What else do you like to eat?

"Pizza. Hot dogs," was the answer and Lily added, "I like macaroni and cheese.

Only I'm tired of the macaroni and cheese at school. I don't like their food."

"Why don't you take your lunch, then?" asked Emma Grace.

"I don't have a lunch box," was the concerned reply.

"Well, I guess we'll have to get you one," she replied.

After breakfast, which came in stages and lasted until almost noon, Emma Grace, Lily, Emily, and Wyatt headed for town to get lunch boxes. Luke was too big and old to need a lunch box, so he stayed behind to shadow his uncle.

By the time the four of them arrived at Wal-Mart, she discovered that none of the children had lunch boxes, backpacks, or much in the way of school supplies. By the time the four of them left Walmart, they all had lunch boxes, backpacks, and lots and lots of school supplies, even Luke whether he wanted those things or not.

Chapter 16

Life at the Wagner Ranch began to fall into a routine, appreciated by some, unappreciated by others.

The ranch and home came to life early in the morning with breakfast, making lunches, and making the thirty plus minute drive to school in town. Emma Grace's day was then filled with what had been unaccustomed tasks of doing laundry, cooking, checking homework, and mothering four children. Hungry stomachs, dirty laundry, and driving kids never seemed to end. Each day finally ended with homework completed and checked, baths, bedtime, a long hot bath for Emma Grace, prayer journal time, and going to bed alone.

The kids seemed to be adjusting all right, especially Emily and Lily. They liked having a "mother" around and the stability she brought to the ranch. Even Wyatt warmed up to her because he liked the three solid meals a day.

However, Luke was a different story. Being the oldest at thirteen and remembering his mother better than his brother and sisters, Luke was not accepting Emma Grace, this family business, or anything that came close to upsetting his previous life. He had been closer to his dad than the others and had a harder time dealing with his death. He also idolized his Uncle Alec and resented anyone he perceived as a threat to his relationship with him.

Chapter 17

Sunday was coming again, and Emma Grace dreaded it. She hated feeling that way, but she knew the argument and fight that would come when expecting Luke to go to church.

It was the middle of a Saturday afternoon and Alec was in the ranch office where he spent most of his time. Emma Grace quietly poked her head in the office doorway.

"Hey, Alec, got a minute?" she asked. She was in unfamiliar territory. She felt comfortable enough in the house, but out here in the barn and office, she still felt out of place and even unwelcomed. But it had become harder and harder to catch Alec at the house. It seemed as though he spent all of the waking hours anywhere on the ranch but the house. Things were usually pretty quiet on the ranch on Saturdays; most of the ranch hands were not around. They were either in the bunkhouse or off the ranch completely, so Emma Grace chose this time and place on purpose.

"Okay. Must be important for you to leave the house and come out here to the ranch office."

"I don't want the kids to hear this conversation. Ummm…I need to talk to you about going to church on Sundays."

Without looking up, Alec roughly replied, "Not going."

"I know you're not a church-going kind of person, but I'm not referring to you. I'm referring to Luke."

"Luke's old enough to make his own decisions. If he doesn't want to go to church, he doesn't have to,"

I'm going to disagree," came the not so quiet Emma Grace. "We agreed that we were getting married to keep the children here at their home and to provide them with a stable and loving home. Going to church, learning about God, trusting Jesus, is part of that. It is a non-negotiable for me."

Alec stopped and looked up from the desk; he set his intense look with his soft blue-gray eyes on her.

She started to buckle. When Alec looked at her that way, it was all she could do to steady herself and breathe normally, but she determinedly stood her ground and fixed her face that said she wasn't backing down. She realized this was probably the first battle between her and her husband, and she wondered which one would break the stare first and back down.

"Okay. He'll go," Alec finally said turning his eyes back to the papers that awaited him on the desk.

"You'll have to step in and make him; he won't go if I tell him to; he'll argue with me."

"Can't you handle a thirteen year old boy?" Alec half-laughingly asked.

"Not Luke, and I know he'll listen to you."

"Okay. I'll talk to him tonight," was the reluctant reply.

The battle took place that Saturday night over grilled hamburgers at the supper table.

"Guys, you need to get to bed a little earlier tonight because tomorrow is church," Emma Grace opened up the conversation.

The three younger kids complained with a few grumblings but finally relented with their okays.

"I don't go to church, so I can stay up later," was Luke's boastful contribution to the conversation.

"I've been meaning to talk to you about that," said Alec, not looking up from his hamburger, "I think you need to go with your brother and sisters."

"But you don't go, Uncle Alec," Luke argued back.

"I know, but I'm grown and you're not."

"You never went to church even when you were my age, and you turned out okay, so I don't know why I have to go."

A long silence while all eyes, including Emma Grace's, were set on Alec as he struggled with an answer.

Finally, "Well, think how much better I'd be if I had gone to church. You're going. End of discussion."

Luke's anger with life and the hand it had dealt him so far finally boiled over and took full aim at Emma Grace with a voice full of loudness, carelessness, and hatefulness. "Doesn't matter. Just because Emma Grace says I should go doesn't mean I have to. She's not my mother, and I don't have to listen to her. She can't tell me what to do. Who does she think she is anyway? She forced her way into this family and our lives. I wish she would go away. I don't want her here. We don't need her. She's such a …

Luke didn't get to finish his hateful sentiments regarding Emma Grace before Alec leaped out of his chair, grabbed Luke by the neck of his t-shirt, and drew back his right arm.

Emma Grace grabbed Alec's arm before his fist made contact with Luke's jaw and shouted, "Stop! That's enough. We don't settle arguments in this house with fist fights. Luke, go upstairs. Kids, go watch TV; you're finished with supper. Alec, sit back down,"

"Kids, do as she says. When she uses that tone of voice, don't argue," came from Alec.

The kids scattered. Alec sat down.

"No one talks to you that way," he finally said.

"I appreciate you taking up for me, and I agree, but you can't hit him. I won't let you. I don't know how arguments were settled before I got here, but we're not doing that. Not while I live here. Do you understand me?"

No answer from Alec.

After a minute or so Emma Grace broke the silence except for the TV from the other room, "Don't you think you should go and apologize to Luke?"

"Why should I apologize? You're the one who wanted Luke to

go to church. I told him to go. He refused and argued with me. I corrected him, and now I'm in trouble and have to apologize?" Alec angrily asked as. "I'm not apologizing. You wanted him to go to church; now he's going."

"Alec, listen." Her tone had changed and now she had returned to the soft and calm Emma Grace. "We can't use force on these kids. They've had a rough few years. We have to be patient; we have to be consistent; we have to have expectations; we have to give consequences; but we also have to give unconditional love at all times. There's got to be a better way than using force. Luke doesn't like me; he doesn't want me here. I understand how he feels. He sees me as replacing his mother and coming in between the two of you, but he still has to have boundaries, and we have to discipline him when he crosses those boundaries. But it can't be by force. Please go upstairs and apologize, but make sure he's going to church tomorrow.

Without replying, he reluctantly went upstairs and knocked on Luke's door.

A quiet, "Come in," answered his knock and Alec walked in. Luke was sitting on the bottom bunk. He wasn't crying, but the tears weren't too far down. Alec sat down beside him and awkwardly and hesitatingly did his best to apologize. He had never apologized before, and this apology business made him uncomfortable.

After a long silence, Alec finally spoke up, "I'm sorry I raised my fist to you. You know I would never do anything to hurt you. The two of us have a special bond, and no one and nothing is going to break that bond. Nothing you can do; nothing I can do; nothing Emma Grace can do to break that. It's special, and I'm sorry for hurting it, but you gotta know you were out of line talking about Emma Grace that way. I don't want you to ever talk that way about her again. Do you understand me?"

A quiet "yes" came from Luke.

Finally, "Do you have anything you want to say?" asked Alec.

"No. Not really."

A nod for Alec followed by another long silence.

"You're still going to church tomorrow.

"But, "Luke began to protest, but stopped abruptly as Alec stood up and started for the door.

"Now, let's go back downstairs, apologize to Emma Grace, and finish our supper."

Supper was gone by the time they got back downstairs, but the offering of lots of ice cream as an olive branch seemed to patch up the special bond between uncle and nephew.

As they were finishing their ice cream and mending the broken bond, Emma Grace walked in with her consequence for Luke and his out of line arguments and comments.

"When you finish your ice cream, you need to copy five times each of these two Bible scriptures: Exodus 20:12 - *Honor your father and mother that your days may be prolonged in the land which the Lord your God gives you* and Ephesians 4:29 - *Let no unwholesome word proceed from your mouth, but only such a word as is good for edification according to the need of the moment, that it may give grace to those who hear.* "After copying those verses, write down in your own words what those verses mean to you."

'No argument from Luke as his uncle watched him. Luke was in the car with Emma Grace and his brother and sisters Sunday morning headed to church.

Chapter 18

"I think you need to pick up the kids early," Alec said one late March morning as Emma Grace was putting chili on in the crock pot for supper. "There's a winter storm coming in later this afternoon, and the road between here and town might become impassable."

"Okay. I'll finish this and head that way."

"Okay, but pay attention to the weather reports. You need to be back home before it hits. I don't want you and the kids to get caught in the storm. I would go, but I have to help button down the hatches here at the ranch."

"Gotcha," was Emma Grace's unworried response.

"I'm serious," was Alec's reply that made her stop and catch his eyes that were filled with concern. "Don't mess around with this storm; it sounds like it's going to be a rough one. I want you back here when it hits."

Emma Grace finished putting the chili on and left to go get the kids. She decided to make a quick run to the grocery store to pick up just a few things because she didn't know how long the storm would last or how long before they would be able to get out and come to town again. By the time she arrived at Luke's school, the car-rider line was longer than she had anticipated; the same was true at the elementary school. It seemed like every parent had the same idea to pick up their children before the storm hit. By the time she was finally able to head home, the storm arrived earlier than expected and hit hard with the howling wind blowing the snow sideways and piling up into drifts that quickly covered the road.

She was inexperienced driving in a snow storm, and she briefly thought about just going to Mr. Wagner's place at the assisted living home to ride out the storm but then she didn't want Alec to think she couldn't handle a snowstorm, so she kept going. The trip home was slow and dangerous with the snow falling so fast that she couldn't tell where the road ended and the ditch began. It wasn't dark, it was just white, a white-out she believed they called it. The snow was blowing toward them, and driving through it was like playing a space video game with lasers (snow flurries) shooting at you.

"Just keep looking at the centerline on the highway," she told herself. However, the centerline quickly disappeared underneath the snow. "We drive off this road, we're not getting back on it," she thought as she tried to keep an eye on the odometer and remember how far apart the twists and turns were.

She looked at the kids in the rearview mirror, and as much unconcern as she could muster in her voice, calmly said, "Wyatt, try to get Uncle Alec on the phone and let him know where we are, and it'll be a while before we get home. Luke, help keep me on the road. You know this road better than me. You know the landmarks, the twists and turns."

Luke squinted hard through the windshield, and Emma Grace tightened her grip on the steering wheel and silently prayed, "Heavenly Father, help me. Show me the way home. I'm claiming your promise ... *'and lo I am with you always.'* In Jesus's name, Amen."

She looked hard out the windshield, and then she heard Luke shout, "Look. Tail lights. Follow them."

"Okay," Emma Grace breathed a little easier seeing the tail lights in front. She checked her rearview mirror and was surprised to see a set of headlights behind her. The two pairs of truck lights seemed to be cradling her, and they made her feel a little safer.

"I'm watching the mileage, and I'll tell you when we should be close to the ranch; then you can start looking for the gate," she told Luke.

The going was slow and tedious, but between her, Luke, and the tail lights in front of them, they were making progress. However, what should have been about a thirty minute ride home was quickly turning into an hour or more.

Alec was back at the ranch pacing back and forth like a corralled wild animal. He was beyond worried, and although he hated to admit it to himself, he was afraid and as always his fear turned into anger.

"That woman," he yelled to Matt. "I told her to be sure and be back here at the ranch before the storm hit. And where is she? Not here."

"The storm hit earlier than we thought, Alec." Matt was trying to calm him down. "It's not her fault. We all thought we had a couple more hours. I'm sure she and the kids are fine. She just has to drive slow. Emma Grace is smart. She wouldn't do anything that would put the kids in danger."

"I don't care. She doesn't know how to drive in this kind of weather. I doubt if she's even driven in a snowstorm before. It's a white-out. She won't know where the road is, much less where the curves are. She's not even going to be able to see where to turn in at the ranch. I should have gone. I knew better. I was more worried about weather-proofing the ranch and livestock."

Silence for a minute, and then Alec tried the phone again. No connection.

"I'm going to take the truck down to the road, so maybe they can see us and know where to turn in."

"I'm coming with you," was Matt's reply.

Emma Grace's eyes were beginning to burn from straining so hard and shifting them back and forth between the truck's tail lights in front of her and the tire tracks he left for her. Every now and then she looked up in the rearview mirror to keep an eye on the eighteen-wheelers' headlights following her. She felt like he was right behind her to make sure she didn't stray off the road. Finally the odometer said they should be getting close to the ranch.

"Okay, Luke, we should be getting close. Keep looking out your window for the gate."

Alec and Matt sat in the truck straining to see anything that would drive by, but there was nothing. The storm had stopped all traffic. Finally, they spotted the black suburban, and Alec let out an uncharacteristic relief, "Thank you, God."

Emma Grace glanced in the rearview mirror and noticed all three kids in the back were helping as much as their little eyes would let them. Four pairs of young eyes along with hers were staring out the front windshield in dead silence.

All five in the car jumped and screamed as the silence was broken by the startling horns of both the front and rear trucks that sounded at the same time. Luke hollered, "I see it. I see it. I see Uncle Alec's truck."

"Yes!" were the combined shouts of jubilation from the back seat.

The suburban slowly turned onto the snow-covered ranch road. Alec jumped out of his truck and ran to the driver's side of the suburban, climbed in, and pushed Emma Grace over. He drove the rest of the ranch road to the house while Matt drove to the bunkhouse.

Chapter 19

As they got to the house and began to pile out of the car, Emma Grace picked up the few bags of groceries and carried them in.

"Woman, what is that, and what are you doing?" His voice was cold, angry, and loud.

"I'm putting up groceries," Emma Grace responded uneasily, detecting the anger in his voice.

"I told you to go get the kids and come right back. Do you know what could have happened? You could have easily driven off the road. You could have been in an accident. You could have killed yourself. You could have killed the kids. You could have been stranded and frozen to death. What you did was foolish and irresponsible. I told you to pay attention to the weather. I told you to be home before the storm hit. You have no experience driving in a blizzard. I never said to stop and run errands. I said to go straight there and straight back. You risked yours and the children's lives. You could have gotten stuck out there and frozen to death."

The more he talked, the angrier he became as if voicing his fears out loud made them more real. He was getting louder, repeating himself, and clenching his fists.

"Enough," Emma Grace shouted back to get his attention and to make him stop all of his ranting and raving. He stopped in mid-sentence, shocked and speechless at her loudness.

Getting in his face and glaring into his angry blue-gray eyes, she quite loudly and decisively said, I'll be upstairs waiting for you to apologize. Otherwise, you can go to the barn and stay there. Kids, grab a snack and go watch some TV for a while." She turned and defiantly and confidently walked upstairs. Once she was behind the closed door to her bedroom, the tears and the uncontrollable shaking came.

As she laid there curled up on the bed with her mascara tears running onto the bedspread, all the fears and doubts about everything rushed through her mind so disjointedly she couldn't find the words to pray.

"God, help me," was all she could come up with in her mind.

"God, help me;" "God, help me," she cried to herself over and over until the shaking slowed, the tears stopped, and the thoughts made more sense.

"Heavenly Father, I know I heard you say to marry Alec and take care of these kids. I know without a doubt this is the path you've put me on, but this is so hard. I can't do this. I am scared; I am lonely; I am doubtful; I don't think things are getting better. Help me. Talk to me. Let me hear your voice." And then out of the blue she remembered Psalm 56: 3, *"When I am afraid, I will put my trust in you."*

The silence was deafening after Emma Grace suddenly walked out of the kitchen, up the stairs, and not so quietly shut the bedroom door. Luke, Wyatt, Emily, and Lily didn't say anything, and neither did they make a move for a snack; they just stared at Alec. Reality began to creep over him. What did he just say to her, or had he yelled at her? Did he really say all that in front of the kids? As the realization of what had just happened flooded over him, the regret of his words towards her was close behind, and behind the regret came the knowledge he had to apologize. Apologizing was not Alec's strong suit. Apologies were a sign of weakness. In fact, the one and only time he could remember apologizing was to Luke for almost hitting him, and that was at Emma Grace's insistence. Now he was going to have to apologize to Emma Grace.

"Kids, do as Emma Grace said. Get a snack and watch TV for a while."

Alec gently and quietly as he could walked up the stairs, took a deep silent breath at the door, and softly knocked. No answer ... "Emma Grace, I'm sorry ... Can I come in?"

A quiet "yes" came from behind the door.

Alec slowly opened the door and saw Emma Grace sitting on the bed. One look at the rumpled bed, the messed up hair, the tear-stained face, and the tear-filled eyes, and he knew he had hurt her horribly. He didn't know what to say other than that he was sorry.

But Emma Grace had plenty to say. "First of all, don't ever call me names. I am not foolish. I am not irresponsible. Second of all, never talk to me like that; ever; but especially in front of the kids. If we have a disagreement, we discuss it in private, not in front of them. Third of all, you never tell me what to do. Besides, you never said go straight there and come straight home. You said keep an eye on the weather, which is what I did. I had the radio on. I was listening to the weather updates, the car-rider lines at the schools were very long, and the storm arrived early and with more of a vengeance than was predicted. Yes, it was dangerous driving in that blizzard, but I had to keep going; I couldn't stop; I couldn't turn around in the middle of the highway. I was watching the mileage so I would know approximately where the turn-off was to the ranch, and Luke was looking out for landmarks. And then there was the truck right in front of me whose tail lights and tracks on the road I followed. And there was the other truck behind me to save us if we did drive off the road. In fact, they both must have recognized the car because they both honked when we came to the ranch turn-in."

Alec stared at her in disbelief. "Emma Grace, you were the only car on the road. There was no truck ahead of you, and there was no truck behind you. Matt and I were in the pick-up at the highway for a good fifteen to twenty minutes before we saw you. There were no other cars, trucks, or anything on the road but you."

"No. You're wrong," she said. "Ask Luke and the kids. In fact ... Luke was the one who first spotted the truck's tail lights and told me to follow them."

"Luke," Alec hollered downstairs, "come up here for a minute." Luke came up the stairs and stood at the doorway to the room.

"How did you manage to stay on the road and get back home?" Alec gently asked.

Breathing a sigh of relief that Alec had calmed down, Luke proudly said, "Driving slowly, following the tail lights from the truck in front of us, and me watching for landmarks."

"There was a truck in front of you?"

"Yeh. I saw it first and told Emma Grace to follow it. I did the right thing, didn't I?" Luke asked, seeking approval from his uncle.

"You did," Alec said and smiled at him. "Good job. I'm proud of you for looking out for Emma Grace and your brother and sisters."

"Thanks," Luke quickly responded with a proud smile and bounded back down the stairs to the TV.

"I swear, Emma Grace, there were no other vehicles of any kind on the road except for your car," Alec said, trying to convince himself of something he already knew.

"You can ask Matt."

Emma Grace responded with a smile on her face and silently whispered, "Thank you, Heavenly Father, for You and your good and faithful word," but out loud with the corners of her mouth turned up said, "Maybe I should give you some Bible verses to copy."

"Not going to happen," was the reply.

Chapter 20

After a very quiet but emotionally noisy dinner of chili that night, the kids picked out two movies to watch. The snow was still falling and the wind was still howling; it was not a night anybody would want to be outside. Everyone, including Emma Grace quickly took their baths, put the pajamas on, and picked a spot with their blankets and pillows to settle down and watch the movies. By the end of the second movie everyone had fallen asleep except for Alec and Luke.

"Luke," Alec whispered, "get your brother up off the floor and you two go on to bed. I'll take the girls up."

But Alec was stuck. At some point during the evening, Emma Grace must have forgiven him for he found her asleep against his arm with Lily asleep in her lap. Emily was asleep on his lap. He turned his face towards Emma Grace and lightly kissed the top of her head. (She smelled so good, just like jasmine.) She stirred, sat up, and gave him a sleepy smile.

"Movie over?" she whispered. "I guess I fell asleep. I'll help you take the girls upstairs."

"That's all right. I got them."

"Okay," and she went upstairs. Alec tucked the last one into bed, and as he passed Emma Grace's room, she quietly called out to him.

He walked in and saw her sitting up in bed still half asleep.

"Look, Alec. Does that remind you of anything?" and she

nodded her head toward the window as she slid back under the covers.

Alec looked out the window and saw a full moon hanging in a fresh clear sky left in the wake of the storm. The moon's brightness was casting dark life-like shadows of trees and far-off mountains on seemingly endless and lonely white blanketed pastures. He stared at the mesmerizing scene remembering a night very much like this one that he and Emma Grace had shared in his hospital room. "I remember. How could I forget?" he finally said and turned towards Emma Grace, but she had already fallen back asleep. He silently stood in her room for some time turning his blue-gray eyes on Emma Grace as she peacefully slept and then turning them back through the window to the cold snow-covered outside world. Today had proven to him what he had long suspected but didn't want to admit. He was in love and afraid.

Chapter 21

"Let's go to the pool," Lily asked one morning shortly after summer had arrived. Summertime at the ranch, and the kids were home from school.

"We'll see," was Emma Grace's half-hearted reply. "Uncle Alec and Luke leave today for a rodeo in Laramie. I need to see what they need from me today before they leave. Probably nothing, but I need to ask anyway. Not much had changed since that night of the snowstorm. She thought about that day a lot; the terrifying ride home in the snowstorm, the anger thrown at her by Alec for putting her and the kids in danger, the doubts about the marriage, the apology from him, and then the softness in his kiss, the beauty after the snowstorm, and the reassuring presence of him in her bedroom. But then within half a heartbeat Alec turned back to his old self. He spent more time in the ranch office or barn than he did in the house. And the doubts began to creep back.

"Let's go, Luke," hollered Alec.

"Ready," came the answer as Luke bounded down the stairs skipping every other step and throwing himself off the porch as he jumped into the truck.

"Wait," said Emma Grace. "Here are some chocolate chip cookies for the ride."

"Thanks," and Alec took them from her hand and headed for the truck.

Emma Grace followed him with her eyes until he stopped

halfway to the truck and turned around. He looked at her with that look that always made her catch her breath.

He hurriedly walked back to her. "Sorry," and he kissed her lightly on the lips. She wanted to throw her arms around him, kids watching and all; she didn't care. Let the kiss linger, she wished. It didn't, but it was still a kiss.

"Be careful," she yelled at them as they backed out. Alec honked the horn and tipped his hat to her. There was still hope.

Life didn't slow down for the Wagners during summer with swimming lessons for Emily and Lily, baseball practices and games for Wyatt, and local youth rodeos for Luke; Emma Grace found it harder and harder to find time for her prayer journal and talks with God. During the school year with bedtimes early and set in stone, she could always count on time with God before bed. Plus, the empty house during the day always provided the quiet Emma Grace wanted and needed to talk to God. But now with the kids running in and out of the house all day and later bedtimes, the prayer journal time and talks with God seemed to be fewer and shorter, and the hope for love to grow between her and Alec began to slip away.

Two nights before Matt and Ashley's wedding in late June, the Wagners along with Matt and Ashley were eating dinner at their favorite Mexican food restaurant. The conversation between Emma Grace and Ashley was mostly about the wedding. Ashley was slowly taking Liz's place as Emma Grace's friend and confidante. Liz lived in Florida and her life was taking her on a separate journey. Ashley was here, her fiance was Alec's best friend who lived and worked on the ranch. Alec, Matt, and Ashley had been friends forever it seemed to Emma Grace; the three of them shared a lot of memories and stories. Without ever talking about it, Emma Grace thought Ashley always went out of her way to make Emma Grace feel like she belonged; that she wasn't an outsider.

At the end of dinner, the kids went out to play on the restaurant's playground, but Lily needed to go to the bathroom. Emma Grace took her. On their way out the bathroom door, Scarlett, along with her friend, busted into the bathroom blocking the exit. One quick look at her and Emma Grace recognized the big hair, big red lips, and the large chest, and she immediately remembered her from Alec's hospital stay. "Do not allow Scarlett Dayton in Alec's room," was written on Alec's chart.

"Hi, Lily," Scarlett, so friendly-sounding, greeted Lily, "Do you remember me? I'm Scarlett, your uncle's girlfriend."

"Yes, but now Uncle Alec is married to Emma Grace, so I guess you're not the girlfriend anymore."

"So I've heard. How's your uncle?"

"Good."

"What are you doing?"

"I'm going outside to play."

"Run along and tell your uncle I said 'hi.'"

Emma Grace started to walk out behind Lily, but Scarlett's friend blocked the door, and Scarlett grabbed Emma Grace by the arm.

"Excuse me, I'm trying to get out," Emma Grace politely said and jerked her arm free from Scarlett's hold.

"Not yet. I've got some things to say to you."

"I remember you from the hospital. The notes on Alec's chart said you were not allowed to see him. We don't see those instructions on someone's chart very often, so I'm guessing he doesn't like you very much and doesn't want you around. And if that's true, then there's nothing you have to say to me that I want to hear, so please let me by."

"I've got plenty to say, and you're not leaving till I do. Alec and I have a long history together, and we were engaged until you came along and put your nose in where it wasn't invited. You took advantage of him when he was sick and needed help with Tom's kids. Now it's time for you to move on. I was out at the ranch the other day and saw Alec. He said he doesn't love you. He's ready to divorce you and get back with me. Everyone knows why you married him. You just want the money from the Wagner family. I bet if you're really nice, he'll pay you a good sum to divorce him and leave. He's my man; not yours."

Emma Grace felt the color uncontrollably drain from her face, and she knew the shaking was about to start. "Keep it together," she told herself. "Do not let this woman know she's having an effect on you. Clear the fears out of your eyes. Put your game face on and put the fierceness in your eyes and voice."

"Excuse me again. Let me out, or I will shout until someone hears me."

Just then someone unsuccessfully pushed on the door from the other side and when it didn't open, they knocked. Scarlett's friend stepped away from the door, and as Ashley walked in, Emma Grace rushed past her out the door. Ashley took one look around the room and caught Scarlett's eye.

"Hello, Ashley," Scarlett said coolly.

"Scarlett," and Ashley knew immediately what happened.

Scarlett's words and accusations shook Emma Grace to the core. "Was Scarlett right? Heaven knows, she and Alec weren't intimate; maybe he was secretly seeing Scarlett. They did have a past together. Maybe Alec was just using her to help raise the kids. Maybe her dreams were just that; dreams. Maybe she didn't really hear God. What have I done? Don't cry. Don't cry," she told herself. "Just get home and get by yourself." In a haze, she stumbled back to the table and sat down. Looking at Alec, she said, "I think it's time to go."

"Everything ok?" he asked. Her voice sounded shaky.

"Sure. It's just getting late. I think I'll go wait outside with the kids on the playground while you get the check and pay," and she picked up her purse and left.

"Okay. Be there in a minute," Alec hollered after her.

"Where did Emma Grace go?" Ashley asked, coming back to the table and sitting down.

"She's outside with the kids while I pay. She's ready to go."

Something's brewing," Ashley said. "Scarlett and her friend were holding Emma Grace hostage in the bathroom. I tried to get in the bathroom, but they were blocking the door so Emma Grace couldn't leave."

"What?" exploded Alec.

Evidently Scarlett and her friend have been sitting somewhere in the back. When they saw Emma Grace and Lily walk into the bathroom, they ambushed her.

"Where was Lily?"

"They let Lily go and she went outside to play. I knew something was up when I saw Scarlett and her friend go into the bathroom after Lily and Emma Grace."

"And you didn't stop them?"

"I didn't think they would do anything with Lily around, but when I saw Lily leave and Emma Grace wasn't with her, I got there as fast as I could."

"Do you know what she said to her?"

"No, but I can imagine. Emma Grace was white as a ghost when she came out of there."

"I'll kill that woman. I have told her a million times to leave me alone, but now she's gone after my wife," and he kicked his chair back while his searing eyes searched the room for Scarlett. He found her, and all the horses on the ranch couldn't stop him from making a beeline to her.

Matt was close behind him and grabbed him before his fist reached Scarlett.

"Let's go," Matt demanded.

"You come near my wife, my kids, my family ever, and you will live to regret that. Do you hear me?" Alec thundered to Scarlett loud enough for the entire restaurant to hear. On his way out, he turned over the closest empty table he could find.

In the car, a seething Alec searched Emma Grace's face for any kind of indication of what happened in the bathroom. Nothing. Blank. She kept her eyes from him until she finally asked, "Could you please stop by the store? I need to pick up a couple of things."

As Alec pulled into the parking space, "What do you need? I'll go in and get it for you."

"No. I got it," she replied, and the car door closed on the "got it." In a few minutes, she returned with two bottles of wine in a grocery sack.

On the way home, Alec slipped his hand over to hers. He felt it shaking before she quickly pulled it away.

"I'm really not feeling well, so I think when we get home, if you could please take care of the kids, that would be great. I'm going to take a long hot bath and go to bed."

"Sure."

Chapter 22

Before Alec could bring the car to a complete stop in the driveway, Emma Grace was out of the car and walking up to the house. She stopped by the kitchen, picked up a corkscrew and a wine glass, and hurriedly walked up the stairs, and slammed the bathroom door shut.

She knew she needed to talk to God, to surrender everything to him, but she was so hurt and so betrayed. "How could I make this same mistake again?" she asked herself. "How foolish can I be? I thought I heard you, God. I believe this is what you want me to do, but it's too hard. I can't do this anymore. " She ran a tub of hot water with lots of bubbles, turned her music on, and pulled herself the first of several glasses of wine.

She didn't know how long she had been in the bathtub, how many glasses of wine she had drunk, how many times she had let the water out and filled the tub again with hot water and bubbles, and then a soft knock at the door.

"Emma Grace, you okay?"

"Yeh. I'm fine. Why?"

"You've been in there a long time, and I think we should talk."

"I don't have anything to say right now, but if you want to talk, come on in."

"Not while you're taking a bath."

"Why not? Last time I checked, we are married, or have you forgotten?"

"No, I've not forgotten, but I can't talk to you when you're in the tub."

Well then we won't talk because I'm not getting out any time soon."

"Come on, Emma Grace, ... then let me in."

"Come on in; the door's not locked. I've never locked a door between you and me."

Alec opened the door and stared at the floor. After finding his courage, he lifted his eyes from the floor and searched for her in the candlelit bathroom that smelled of jasmine. They finally settled on her in the bathtub covered in bubbles with her hair piled on top of her head and her beautiful tear-stained face turned towards him with her tear-filled eyes staring at him. He couldn't read what they were saying; there was a coldness to them, but he also detected a hurt pleading from them.

"We need to talk," he said while his eyes searched the bathroom and landed on an almost empty bottle of wine with a full glass beside it. "I'm not sure this is the right place to do that."

Well, then talk to yourself somewhere else; I'm not leaving."

"How long are you going to be in here?"

"Till I can drink enough to forget what happened tonight."

Alec leaned against the wall next to the bathtub and slid to the floor with his knees bent toward his chest. until he stretched them out before him on the cold bathroom floor. He quietly moved the wine bottle from her reach and said, "I think you've had enough."

"Nope. I can still remember."

"I thought you would take what happened and pray to your God about it"

"I wish I could, but I can't right now. I am too angry and hurt. I don't know what to say to Him."

"Then let's talk about it. Are you angry with me?"

"Yes, but I'm more angry with myself. I can't believe I've made the same mistake with you as I did with Will."

"Come on, Emma Grace. Please don't think I'm like that guy. I won't hurt you. Let's at least talk about what happened."

"You already have. I don't think there's anything you can say now. What's done is done. What's been said, has been said. I've made the same mistake I made before. I believed you; I believed in you just like I believed in Will. After all of my praying; after all my seeking God and believing I had found Him and trying so hard to walk with Him; to put Him first; to read His Word; to listen for Him. I know I heard Him and felt Him. I heard Him bless us; bless this union; bless this family. But then you go and tell that woman you want to divorce me and be with her …"

He interrupted her. "Emma Grace, that's not true. I never told her anything like that. I don't want that. I can't believe you believed her."

"Why wouldn't I believe her? We're not exactly close, if you know what I mean. You still sleep on the sofa downstairs, and I sleep up here. In fact, I always feel like you're trying to avoid me. I don't know what else I can do to help this marriage and to make this family a family that loves each other. I keep thinking we just need more time. And maybe we do, but you're not going to give this family that time, are you?"

"Yes I am, I'm in this forever. I'm not going anywhere; I don't want you going anywhere."

"Then why did she say that?"

"Because that's what she does. She's toxic. We did have a relationship, if you want to call it that, a long time ago. The last time I was with her was before the accident., before I knew you. You know she tried to see me in the hospital but wasn't allowed. There was a reason for that. I don't like her. I don't want her anywhere around me or you or the children."

"She said she was here at the ranch the other day. Is that true?"

"She was, but I had her thrown off, and I immediately went to the sheriff's office and filed a restraining order on her. She cannot come anywhere on this ranch or within five hundred feet of it. You can check, if you don't believe me. That's why she went after you at the restaurant; she can't get to you here. I'm going to go tomorrow and have a restraining order filed against her coming anywhere near you or the kids. I'll have plenty of witnesses. Ashley will testify to what happened in the bathroom. Lily will also, if we need her to. And then there's all the people in the restaurant."

"What do you mean?" and her questioning eyes met his concerned-filled eyes.

"After you went outside, Ashley told me they wouldn't let you out of the Ladies Room, and knowing Scarlett, I could imagine what she told you, so I went to threaten her if she ever came near you or the children again.. If Matt hadn't stopped me, I would have hit her. I did manage to threaten her if she ever came near my wife or children again."

Silence, and finally, "Did you call me your wife...in public?

"Yes, and I meant it. I won't allow anyone to threaten my wife and children."

"She may get a restraining order against you."

"She might and that's just fine."

"Why didn't you tell me about her and the restraining order?"

"I don't know. I thought I had taken care of it."

"You mean, you didn't trust me, did you?"

"It has nothing to do with trust."

Silence again, but then hesitantly Alec continued, "I think somewhere inside me, I thought you might leave if you knew there was some kind of threat, so I didn't say anything."

"You don't want me to leave?"

"No. Never. Why would you think that?"

"Because you keep me at a distance. It seems like we were closer when you were in the hospital ... before we were married. Maybe getting married was a mistake."

"Do you really believe that?"

"I don't know. I don't know what to think anymore."

"I understand. And I'm sorry for keeping you at such a distance. But … you scare me … I mean my feelings for you scare me," and Alec took his fear-filled eyes off the floor and found Emma Grace's eyes as he continued, "I am not the man I was when I first met you. You have changed me. You and the kids are my life now. I love you and the kids and our life. I don't want you to leave. I think sometimes I live in fear that you will discover what kind of man I was and leave. I don't want that."

A silence fell in the bathroom again as Emma Grace played with the faucet with her toe and took a long sip of wine draining her glass. Alec shifted his eyes between searching her face and eyes for a clue as to what she was thinking and then looking at the floor afraid of what he might see in those now crystal clear green eyes.

Breaking the silence, Emma Grace said, "I think I need some water. Would you go get me a bottle of water, please?"

"Sure, but don't try to get out of the tub. I'm afraid you'll fall. Wait till I get back."

She nodded.

Emma Grace was passed out on the bed when Alec walked back upstairs. He stared at her for a while, pulled back the sheets and quilt, tucked her under the covers, and removed the towel and the hair clip from her hair. He sat next to her on the bed while stroking her hair before he went back downstairs, locked up, turned out the lights, and went back upstairs.

"God, help me to know what to do. I don't want to lose her," he whispered to himself as he made himself as comfortable as he could in the chair in her bedroom and tried to sleep. He was going to be there if she got sick or needed help.

Chapter 23

Emma Grace slept late the next morning, and the kids were already fed and off doing whatever they usually did on summer mornings. Alec was sitting at the kitchen table drinking coffee when she walked into the kitchen still wearing yesterday's makeup and feeling a little unstable and foggy.

Alec looked up from the papers he was working on, stared at her, and with a grin cheerfully said, "Good morning, Sunshine. How do you feel on this lovely morning?"

"Mmmmmm," was the grunt. "I've felt better."

"I imagine so. Drinking a whole bottle of wine by yourself can't feel good." What were you thinking?"

"I really don't want to talk about it now. I need some Advil and my hot tea."

Alec sat there silently and watched her down a bottle of water with Advil, make her tea, and slowly sit down.

"Do you remember much about last night?"

"I remember that horrible Scarlett and the things she said. I remember the wine and the bubble bath. I kinda remember us talking in the bathroom but don't remember what was said; anything after that, I don't remember at all."

"Well, that's too bad. We made love last night, and it was great. The best. Sorry you don't remember. It was earth-shattering," he said, staring straight into her confused green eyes with his laughter-filled eyes as a smile slowly curled up the corners of his mouth.

"That's not nice," she smiled and tossed a dish towel at him.

"Well, maybe that's not true, but I did see you naked," and he smiled and winked at her.

"That's okay. I still saw you naked before you saw me naked," Emma Grace teasingly replied with a wink.

Alec gathered up some papers, refilled his coffee cup, kissed her lightly on the cheek, and headed for the back door when he almost ran into Matt who came bursting through the door.

"Sorry to interrupt, but that mountain lion struck again early this morning; got a calf."

"You sure?" asked Alec.

"Yeh. Just like the last. Some of the boys said they heard him really early this morning. They waited till daylight to go after him. That's when they found his handiwork. Same as last time"

"I thought he had moved on," Alec answered, "onto Baker's ranch. They've lost a couple of young calves."

"Yes. A lot of ranchers have."

"Saddle up. I'll get my rifle and meet you."

"Can I go too?" asked Luke running in behind Matt with excitement and anticipation.

"Nope."

"Please?" but the plea was ignored as the back door slammed shut behind Alec leaving Emma Grace to deal with the fallout.

"That's not fair. I never get to do anything. I'm just as old as he was when he started riding bulls, and Grandpa told me he got a gun when he was ten. I'm almost fourteen, don't have a gun, and can't ride bulls. He doesn't spend time with me anymore. He doesn't care about me. All he cares about is this ranch. I hate him and this place," and he stomped off to his room upstairs.

Emma Grace sighed and thought, "Here we go again; I don't think I've got the energy to deal with him this morning," and she decided to let Luke simmer down some before she confronted him; that behavior and talk were not tolerated.

After a while and time enough for Luke to simmer down, Emma

Grace hoped, she knocked on Luke's bedroom door, "Luke, may I come in?"

"No," he shouted back; he hadn't simmered down any.

"Luke, we need to talk about this. I prefer you open the door and let me in."

"No. Stay out of my room. This isn't your house. You're not my mom. I don't have to listen to you. And Uncle Alec's not my dad. I don't have to listen to him either. Just leave me alone."

Emma Grace threw open the door. Without saying a word and without taking her eyes off Luke, as calmly as she could, she grabbed the cell phone off his bed and unhooked the keyboard from the computer. Luke jumped up from the bed and rushed towards her.

"You lay one hand on me, and it will be the last thing you ever do in this house. I promise you that. I know you're mad at your uncle right now, but I also know how much you love and respect him. That relationship will be gone forever if you strike out at me."

"What are you gonna do? Tell on me? Tattle-tale?"

"Your actions and words right now are doing nothing but proving you are indeed too young and immature to go hunting that mountain lion with the men. You just sit in her and think about how childish and selfish you're being. She left but returned shortly with a Bible, some paper, and a pencil.

"Here. Write each of these verses five times and then explain them in your own words," were her directions.

Luke looked at them: Psalm 19:14 - *Let the words of my mouth and the meditation of my heart be acceptable in Thy sight, O Lord, my rock and my Redeemer;* Proverbs 29:11 - *A fool always loses his temper, But a wise man holds it back.;* Psalm 37:8 - *Cease from anger, and forsake wrath; Do not fret, it leads only to evildoing.*

"I will not."

"Okay. It's your funeral," and she walked out carrying the cell phone and keyboard. She left the door open, but heard it slam behind her.

By the time Alec and the rest of the ranch hands returned to the barn, he found Emma Grace in the barn saddling up Dolly.

"Any luck?" she asked.

"No. He's probably long gone or holed up for the day in some remote out cropping. Where are you going?"

"Just for a ride. Luke and I got into it again, and I need some distance."

"What was it about this time?"

"Same old; same old. He resents me and doesn't like me being around, but now he also doesn't like you because you wouldn't take him with you to hunt that mountain lion. He got mouthy, so I took his phone and keyboard and told him to stay in his room. He is supposed to be copying some Bible verses, but he refused. So, he can stay there until he gets them copied."

"You would think he would know the entire Bible by now seeing how he has to copy Bible verses every time he gets in trouble."

"You would think so, but right now I need to cool down, think, and talk to God; He and I have a lot to talk about, so I'm going riding. It will also put some distance between Luke and me for a while."

"Okay. Go ahead, but take Wyatt with you. I'll deal with Luke."

"Can you wait? I'd rather us deal with him together."

"Okay, but don't go yet." Alec walked towards the house and hollered for Wyatt who hollered back, "What?" and came running out slamming the screen door behind him.

"Saddle up and go with Emma Grace to check some of the fencing." Alec said with a tone that Wyatt knew he had no choice but to go.

As Wyatt and Emma Grace were mounted and headed away from the barn, Alec hurriedly rushed after them carrying the first firearm he could get his hands on, an old rifle that had a hard kick to it which he forgot in his hurry.

"Take this. I don't think you'll need it since it's just after noon and most everything is seeking shelter against the sun and napping, but that mountain lion may still be lurking around. Check the fencing, but stay close to the house.

Emma Grace took the rifle and slipped it into the scabbard. She gave a forceful "ticktick," briskly kicked Dolly's sides, and trotted off with Wyatt riding up beside her.

Alec watched them for a minute and turned to go back to the barn. He stopped for a minute and stared at the house. He thought about going after Luke, but didn't. There was work to be done in the office, but he caught a glimpse of Matt at the side corral and walked towards him. He put one foot up on the bottom rail, folded his sunburnt and weathered arms over the top rail, and set his stubbled chin on his arms. "What are you still doing here? Aren't you getting married in a couple of days? I thought Ashley would be ordering you around right about now," he teased Matt.

"Yeah, right. Like she's gonna trust me to do anything with the wedding. All I know is I'm getting married. She tells me where and when I'm supposed to be and what I'm to wear. I'm out here working because it keeps me from getting nervous," Matt answered back as he walked towards Alec. Matt reached the fence and mirrored the same pose as Alec.

"Yeh, I think you're supposed to be a little nervous before you marry," Alec replied.

"Were you?"

"I don't get nervous," was the flat reply. "Besides, my wedding happened so fast, who had time to get nervous?"

"Oh, don't deny it, Alec. I know you were nervous before marrying her, and I also remember how you swore your whole life that you would never marry. Everyone knows you got married to keep Tom's kids here at the ranch instead of moving them to Arizona. What no one can understand is why she agreed to marry you. At first we all thought she was marrying for the money, but then it turned out she has more money than you. Then we all thought maybe she married you for the fame, you being the American Bull Rider of the Year and all, but all that's gone away and she's still here.

111

So, that only leaves that maybe she really cares about you; otherwise, why would she marry a skinny, scarred, mean cowboy like you?"

Alec straightened up leaving one foot on the bottom rung, pushed his hat back from his forehead, and resumed his previous position with his arms folded on the top rail and his chin set on his arms.

After a while.

"That's just it," Alec said seriously and the lines in his wrinkled forehead burrowed deeper.

"I've asked myself that question a hundred times a day ever since we've been married. Why would she want to marry me? I'm nothing but an old broken-down, used up cowboy that can't even walk right."

Before Matt could reply, they heard a loud gunshot that shattered the midday quiet and stillness. They both jumped and froze at the same time. And before the echoes of that shot silenced, another one shattered the midday stillness.

One quick silent exchange with each other and Alec and Matt bolted for the truck and drove at breakneck speed towards the direction of the two shots.

hapter 24

E mma Grace really didn't feel much like talking; she was hurt by the things Luke had said and she wanted time to be by herself, lick her wounds, ask God's forgiveness for the night before, talk to God, and figure out what to do next. She had learned years ago to run towards aloneness when things got out of control and she didn't know what to do. Alone and undisturbed she could think and feel everything. Here on the ranch, she learned to run for the wide-open spaces surrounded by uninterrupted sky and the far-off mountains. She loved this country: the openness, the wildness, the beauty, the ruggedness, and the loneliness. She could breathe, and more importantly, she could see and feel God; it was easier out here, without interruptions, to hear God. She knew out here in the wildness there was danger, but she not only knew God was here; she felt him and knew He would protect her. Besides her prayer journal and talks with God before bed, this is where she met and talked with God. She knew she could talk to God anywhere, but with all the cooking, helping with homework, raising the kids, and running so many errands, it was hard to hear God, but here, in what she believed was God's front yard, she could really listen for him, and she knew she was welcomed. She wanted to cry. She wanted to cry for the hurt Luke had dealt her. She wanted to cry for the disappointment she believed Alec felt in her. She wanted to cry for her weakness last night. She wanted to cry for the beauty of this country. She wanted to cry for the closeness she felt to God. But she couldn't; Wyatt was here.

They rode for quite a while without saying anything. She gave up on trying to have her quiet time with God while Wyatt was with her, so she finally turned to him and gave him a small smile and a forced cheerfulness.

"How are you doing?"

"Good," he replied.

Wyatt slowly opened up to her. He said he was sorry about what Luke had said and for the way he treated her. He talked about being nervous ushering at Matt's wedding. He talked about baseball and how much he liked playing it. Emma Grace listened and nodded every now and then as they continued to ride farther and farther away from the house. Listening to Wyatt was settling to her and helped her put most of her doubts aside for a minute. Somehow listening to an eleven-year-old's life helped her put her life in perspective. And she loved him for it. And she thanked God; He talked to her in mysterious ways.

As she was listening and thinking about everything Wyatt rattled on about, her horse stopped and suddenly snorted and reared up. Emma Grace held the reins firmly and pulled back hard on them. Her heartbeat quickened, and her sun-filled green eyes quickly darted around looking for danger. Her eyes caught a movement and there he unexpectedly was, the mountain lion, about fifty yards up ahead and to the right on top of a boulder.

"Wyatt, freeze," she whispered. "Hold tightly onto the reins. Get ready for him to rear up."

Wyatt followed her stare to the mountain lion and understood.

She quietly and slowly slid off the saddle with the rifle. She didn't really know where to stand and take the shot. She knew Dolly would bolt at the sound of the gunshot, and she didn't want to get trampled. She hoped and prayed that Wyatt could control his horse.

In the time it takes to gasp for a breath, everything she had learned on all the hunting trips she had taken with her dad came back to her. In careful, deliberate slow motion. Steady. Target. Breathe out. One unhesitant motion. Squeeze.

The jolt and the ear-splitting bang landed her on her back on the hard dirt, but before she could think or feel the pain, she jumped back up looking for her target. Dolly took off, but Wyatt managed to hold on to his horse.

"I think you got him," yelled Wyatt.

"Shhh. Where is he?"

"He's down. You shot him clean off that boulder."

Her eyes found the downed mountain lion, but she wasn't sure if he was dead. In careful, deliberate slow motion. Steady. Target. Breathe out. One unhesitant motion. Squeeze. Emma Grace hit the hard dirt again.

Wyatt slid off his horse. "You okay?" he asked.

"Yeh, why?" she asked as she rubbed her shoulder and noticed she was uncontrollably shaking.

Alec, with Matt in the passenger seat, was racing the old red ranch truck across the pasture as fast as it would go, praying that no one was hurt and mad that Emma Grace had not stayed close to the house.

"There's Emma Grace's horse," Matt yelled. " Let me out. I'll get the horse and follow you," said Matt.

Alec finally spotted Wyatt's horse, and a short distance away, he saw them. Wyatt was standing up staring down, and Emma Grace was on the ground.

"Oh God, no!" he screamed silently to himself and pressed down harder on the gas pedal. He sped up close to them, slammed on the brakes, and in a cloud of dirt and dust raced up to them as fast as he could, half expecting Emma Grace to be hurt.

"Everybody ok?" he screamed, afraid to hear the answer.

Wyatt ran towards him grinning and pointing to the mountain

lion, "Emma Grace killed him. Shot him clean through the heart and the neck."

Alec's eyes found the mountain lion lying on the hard ground. Once he was certain the mountain lion was dead, he rushed over to Emma Grace.

"You hurt? You ok?"

"Yeh, I'm fine," was her reply that settled Alec down, and he breathed a sigh of relief.

"Everybody's fine? No one's hurt?" Alec was still not certain everyone was okay, especially himself. Surely this kind of fear left some visible sign of hurt.

"We're all okay except for him," Wyatt joyfully said pointing to the dead mountain lion.

Alec crouched down next to the dead mountain lion just as Matt rode up. They both visually examined the dead animal. Alec pointed to the two gunshot wounds. He and Matt looked at each other and shook their heads in disbelief.

Alec retrieved a shovel from the back of the truck, shoveled up the mountain lion, and threw him in the back of the truck.

Wyatt and Matt rode the horses back, and Alec and Emma Grace rode back in the truck with the dead mountain lion in the bed of the pick-up

Alec was mad at himself for giving her a gun that he knew would knock her over if she fired it, and he was just as mad at her for not staying close to the house like he had asked her. The emotional noise in the truck was deafening, but the physical silence was only broken by the truck racing across the pasture.

Chapter 25

Luke got off easy that day. There was so much commotion over the killing of the mountain lion, that Alec and Emma Grace forgot about why she and Wyatt went for a ride anyway.

Later that evening Emma Grace left the house for the barn. She told Alec she was going to feed Dolly and brush her down, but she really needed her time alone with God. Alone in the stall with Dolly and the quietness of twilight approaching, everything engulfed her at once. Between the fight she was losing to Luke, the uncertainty of her marriage, the fear of the mountain lion, the relief of killing it, and the pain in her shoulder from the kick of the rifle, she finally allowed the tears to come. The day and preceding night had been such an emotional one, and she had held back the tears for so long that when they finally were allowed to come, they came in waves of sobs.

It was okay to cry here all alone. Nothing was required of her here. There were no power struggles, no convincing others to love and accept her, no battles to be fought here in this safe place; there was just a horse who needed feeding and brushing. Just like being out in the open spaces of the Wyoming countryside, here she could also think. Here, she could feel. Here, she could cry. Here, she could ask her questions. And she did what she always did when the rug seemed to be pulled out from under her, and she landed with her face in the dirt. She turned her face up and brought herself to her knees. Now it was just she and her God. The smells of livestock flesh and fresh hay, the silent sun's rays sliding through the slits between the barn's wooden boards with softness, and the twilight mountain aloneness gave her the peace she needed to talk to God. God was here.

"Dear Lord, I know you're here. I smell you in this mountain air; I see you in the beauty of this horse, but I can't hear you; I can't hear the words, 'I've got you back.' I know you do; I just can't hear you. Help me to hear you. I want to hear you. Whisper in my ear, 'I'm with you always.' Holy Spirit, breathe on me. I feel like I've hit a brick wall. Please grant me whatever I need to go through this wall, over it, or around it. I love you; I trust you, but I really need some confirmation that I'm still on the path of your will. Help me. I claim your word in 2 Kings 20:5 - *I heard your prayer. I have seen your tears; behold, I will heal you.* In Jesus's name I pray. Amen."

She didn't know how long she had been there, but soft moonlight rays had now replaced the sun's soft dying rays, and they now slid through the slits between the barn's wooden boards. Without any warning she heard from behind her that familiar raspy, deep, gentle voice that she loved so much, and she did her best to quickly recover from her tears.

"Are you okay?" he asked for the second time in less than twenty-four hours. He didn't want to disturb her, but he was worried; she had been out here in the barn for quite a long time just like last night in the bathroom.

"Yes, I'm fine," she replied, and he limped into the stall and quietly stood on the other side of the horse from her.

She changed her mind. "No, I'm not," she answered as the tears started again. She sat down in the hay, drew her knees up to her chest, wrapped her arms around them, and rested her forehead on her knees, and the sobs returned.

Treading softly through unfamiliar territory and not knowing what else to say, Alec at last broke the sound of the sobs, "Don't tell anyone, but I cried too the first time I killed a deer. It's only natural."

"It's not that," Emma Grace replied, trying to catch her breath and stop the tears.

Silence.

"Then ... what?" asked Alec, really trying hard to be sympathetic and caring.

Between the salty tears and the sobs, it came out of her slowly, hesitatingly, and breathless. "I love this family ... I love Luke, Wyatt, Emily, and Lily ... I love you ... I love our life here. I do. I do. I've never been more sure of anything as sure as I am of this. You and I and this family are as right as church on Sunday morning, but I know how this relationship started. I know you didn't marry me because you love me. I know we don't have a typical marriage. But at the same time, I've never been more sure of anything than this marriage and family. I don't know how I know; I just know it's a God-thing, but ... sometimes it's just so hard ... sometimes I feel like the devil is pulling out all the stops to derail this family.

... Silence ...

Then, between sobs and quite unexpectedly with her face still buried in her drawn-up knees, "I miss my mom and dad, especially Daddy. I was more like him than my mom. He took me hunting with him, and when I was little, he took me to the office with him. He taught me all about hunting and guns. He taught me a little about the oil business, and whenever there was something I wanted, he always supported me. Like, I wanted to go to a public school instead of a private school. My Mother said public schools were for ordinary people, and we weren't ordinary. I wanted to go to Texas A & M instead of the University of Texas; Mom said no one in our family was an Aggie, and it was going to stay that way. I wanted to be a nurse. Mom said over her dead body would she allow a daughter of hers to bathe and clean out bed pans for fat, stinky, old men. Every time, I would go to Daddy. We had this routine. I would show up at Daddy's office unannounced, and his secretary would let me in, and there he would be, sitting behind his too big of a desk in front of a huge window with downtown Houston as his backdrop. He would look up, stop whatever he was doing, and ask what I wanted (There was no small talk with Daddy.). I would tell him, and he would ask, 'Are you sure?' I would answer, 'Yes.' Then he would say 'Okay. Don't worry about your mom. I got your back.' Then he would get up out of his chair, walk around that huge desk and away from the Houston backdrop, give me a hug, and tell me how proud he was of me. I think he liked that I was a little rebellious and went down the unexpected path. I believe he was proud of me, and I think he would be proud of me now. But I want him to ask me what I want now. I want to tell him that I want you to love me as your wife. I want to love you as my husband. I want Luke to stop hating me. I want us to be a loving family that supports each other. I want a family that is Christ-centered. And I want him to tell me 'Okay,' and I want to hear those words, 'I've got your back.' I mean, I know the Lord is with me, and I try so hard to let him direct my path, but sometimes I just need to know that there is someone here who has my back; I need to hear those words.

"I thought your faith in God was enough for you," was Alec's long time in coming answer.

Emma Grace froze for a suspended moment and then lifted her face towards Alec as a smile slowly appeared lighting up her face and eyes. "You're right." She took his hand, brought it up to her lips, and kissed it. "Thank you." They walked back to the house, their shadows from the early softness of the moon following them.

Chapter 26

Wedding day for Matt and Ashley; and Alec had been somewhat dreading this day. Not because he wasn't happy for both of them, after all, he and Matt had been best friends for as long as he could remember, and Matt was so in love with Ashley, but it was customary for the best man to give a toast, and Alec was the best man. If he was uncomfortable in his suit and tie (He could count on both hands the number of times he had worn a tie.), he was more than a little uncomfortable thinking about the best man's toast to the new couple. He had given some thought as to what to say but hadn't written down anything. Was he supposed to be light and humorous, be serious, give advice? He wasn't sure. He knew it had to be special. It had to be truthful and heartfelt. But he was a man of little words.

In spite of the children's arguing and moaning and groaning of having to bathe and get dressed up in their Sunday best in the middle of the day, the Wagner family was finally dressed and driving down the highway to the church in town for Matt and Ashley's wedding.

The wedding ceremony was over, and now the Wagner family was sitting at the dinner reception with the toast looming ever and ever closer. Alec thought about what he was going to say when he felt Emma Grace's hand on his arm and heard her ask, "Are you ready for your toast?"

He turned and set his gaze on her like he had done so many

times before, but this time was different. He knew she was pretty, but tonight seeing her dressed up in her deep purple dress and wearing her diamond earrings that put even more sparkle in those green eyes, with the high-heels that showed off her slender and slightly curvy legs, and her long hair flowing past her shoulders, she was more than pretty and looking at her made him take a long deep breath. His intense and soft blue-gray eyes along with his heart watched her as she cut up Lily's chicken, caught Wyatt's water glass before it spilled, pulled Emily's long hair back from her face, and gave Luke permission to take his tie off.

It was toast time.

Alec rose from his chair and slowly walked up to the front of the room still feeling Emma Grace's hand on his arm. He took the mic, gave a smile and a nod to Matt and Ashley and began.

"Last summer when Matt asked me to be his best man, I was honored … until I learned that the best man is expected to give a toast. And even though I am a man of many words (a soft chuckle rippled through the guests), giving a toast is more frightening than the second before the gate opens and the bull shoots out."

Looking at Matt and giving him a wink, "Who would have thought that I would be toasting you today as a married man? Never in a million perfect bull rides and scores would I have thought I would be here as a married man, with children, honoring you and your bride on your wedding day, but as I have learned from Emma Grace and have more than once experienced myself; God works in mysterious ways.

Matt, you've been like a brother; you HAVE been a brother to me and also to Tom. For as long as I can remember, it was always the three of us: you, me, and Tom. You and Tom were best friends since like the first grade, and y'all let me tag along. I don't know if you felt sorry for me because I was so scrawny or because I was an easy scapegoat for you guys. I don't guess it matters because the three of us, much to the frustration of my dad, your parents, and most of Casper, had a lot of good times and made some really good memories. We also did some things and made some memories that we wish we could undo and never remember again. We have broken horses, broken bulls, broken bones, and broken laws. We have slept in trucks, on the ground, in barns, in bars, and behind bars, and occasionally in our own beds. We rodeoed, rode the circuit, and moved from town to town, always in search of that perfect ride and always having each other's back. You, Matt, literally covered my back everytime a bull threw me ... which was more times than either one of us can count.

Tom was the first one to walk down the aisle, and then it was just the two of us for a short time until Ashley sashayed into our lives. You've been in love with her since junior high, but I never cared for her too much because I thought she was so high and mighty and she would come between us and you wouldn't have my back anymore. But she turned out to be so darn likable, and you proved to be the same friend as you had always been. So, it kind of became the three of us again, except Ashley was more of our rescuer than a participant. How many times, Ashley, have you rescued me from a woman you knew was trouble, but I didn't see it? How many times have you bailed Matt and me out of jail? How many times have you picked us up from bars when we were too drunk to drive? And it was you, Ashley, who was the first one to tell me, 'Emma Grace is the best thing that's happened to you. Don't' blow it.' And you were right again," Alec continued looking directly at Ashley and catching her eyes, "Thank you, Ashley, for all of it."

"Matt," Alec again turned his eyes back to Matt, "Do you remember several years ago when I was at my lowest? I had had one of the worst weeks and worst rides in my career at the Houston rodeo and that started my downward spiral of self-pity and self-loathing. I stayed on the circuit and kept riding even though the scores kept dropping and the rides became shorter. I was taking more and more risks in the arena, foolish risks that could have cost me my life. In fact, it did cost me my walk. I never told you why I still continued to get in the arena and take chances. It wasn't entirely my stubbornness and bull-headednes ... I did it partly because I knew you were there right beside me, and you had my back. I knew that no matter what that bull was going to do to me, you would be there to save me. You would take the bull's attention away from me and turn it on you so I could escape. I can't count how many times you did that for me. And for that, I will always be grateful to you, brother."

A brief pause ...

"God knows, along with everyone in this room, that I am not an expert at this marriage thing, so I'm not sure my advice is the best, but I can tell you what I've learned from listening to and watching Emma Grace. I've learned you've got to respect each other because there will be times when you're so mad at the other, you can lose sight of the love, but not the respect. I know how much you, Matt, love Ashley. I've seen it for years. And I know, Ashley, how much you love Matt. You couldn't put up with his quirks and smelly feet (again a few chuckles rumble through the crowd) if you didn't love him. But I also know that sometimes anger can get in the way of that love. That's when respect comes in. You can't stay angry with someone when you respect and admire them. I know you both respect each other because I"ve seen it. I've seen it when you didn't know I was looking. So, don't forget the respect.

Another piece of advice I want to share with you is to have each other's back, no matter what comes. In the short time I have been married, I have learned that marriage is like that. You and Ashley will go through life together, but every now and then one of you will face a situation, whether it's a fight with one of the kids or some kind of health issue, that will throw you off balance and buck you off. When that happens, the other one steps in and covers your back. That's marriage. You're a team. You have each other's back, and you have to have faith in each other for that.

But perhaps the best advice I can give you is what I've learned from Emma Grace. Not only do you have to have faith in each other, but you have to have faith in a higher being, God. I can tell you from experience that if it weren't for Emma Grace's unrelenting faith in God, she and I would not be together today. She has taught me that unwavering faith gets you through the hard times: rebellious children, anger, health problems, self-loathing, doubts, even killing a mountain lion. I've seen Emma Grace take hits that landed her in the dirt, and I've seen her pull herself up to her knees and turn her face up to God. And somehow or another, He has been there and rescued her. And He has done the same for me more times than I can count, even though I didn't know it. That steadfastness; that faith will get you through anything.

So, Matt, here ends one chapter of our lives. Much to the relief of our parents, those who have known us, and to the law enforcement of Casper, our chapter has come to an end. No longer will we be breaking bones and breaking laws; although, we may still break a horse or bull or two if we can sneak it past the girls. No longer will we be chasing that perfect ride from town to town. We both are starting a new chapter, and you are no longer responsible for having my back. It's now your job to have Ashley's back and Ashley's job to have your back along with faith in God.

"...Like I know Emma Grace has my back, and ... I have Emma Grace's back. With that and our faith in God, we can survive anything. So, here's to Matt and Ashley. I love you both."

Alec takes his eyes off the newly married couple, searches the room for Emma Grace, lands his eyes on Emma Grace's tear-filled eyes, and pushes his way through the cheers to her.

"Let's go home," he whispers.

About the Author

Susan Beard Istre has taught English and United States history for over thirty years in the Texas secondary public school system. She has two adult children and three grandchildren. She is a fifth generation Texan who makes her home in a small Texas town outside of Houston. *Right as Church on Sunday Morning* is her first novel.

Printed in the United States
by Baker & Taylor Publisher Services